Text © Gary Haq 2018

First published in Great Britain in 2018 by GAZZIMODO

www.gazzimodo.com

Cover design and typesetting by Mandy Norman
Cover illustration and chapter heads by Mark Beech

A CIP catalogue record for this book is available from the British Library.

ISBN 978 1 9999337 9 1

This is a work of fiction. Names, places, events and incidents are either the products of the author's imagination or used fictitiously. Any resemblance to actual persons living or dead, or actual events is purely coincidental.

Printed and bound in Great Britain by Lightning Source

MY DAD, THE EARTH WARRIOR

GARY HAQ

Illustrated by Mark Beech

GAZZIMODO

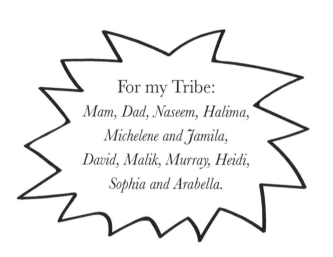

For my Tribe:
Mam, Dad, Naseem, Halima,
Michelene and Jamila,
David, Malik, Murray, Heidi,
Sophia and Arabella.

We have forgotten how to be good guests, how to walk lightly on the Earth as its other creatures do.
BARBARA WARD

The more clearly we can focus our attention on the wonders and realities of the universe about us, the less taste we shall have for destruction.
RACHEL CARSON

You cannot get through a single day without having an impact on the world around you. What you do makes a difference, and you have to decide what kind of difference you want to make.
JANE GOODALL

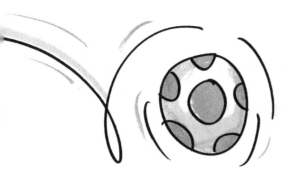

CONTENTS

Heatwave
Blistering Bertha

'But, **Daaaad**, are you sure she's going to be there?' said Hero. It was a sweltering day in July, and they were once again at Leaford International Airport.

'I told you she's arriving this afternoon,' Dad said firmly. He stood at the entrance dressed for the heatwave in his black vest, khaki shorts and Union flag flip-flops – his matchstick legs proudly on display.

'Okay.' Hero nodded, unconvinced that hanging around a stuffy airport listening to Dad witter on about some random fact was the best start to the summer holidays.

He followed Dad into the terminal building. Inside, several old fans creaked away, working hard to make up for the broken air conditioning but failing miserably to keep the place cool.

Hero cringed at the sight of people shading their eyes and slipping on sunglasses as Dad strode ahead, his skinny body a beacon of whiteness in the mass of crimson-faced travellers.

'But did you find out why she's coming back now?' he asked, trying to keep pace.

Dad sighed. 'I still don't know. Her one-line text messages are more cryptic than *The Times* crossword.'

They passed a row of shops before Hero stopped outside the Flying Bean Café. He took off his blue Leaford City baseball cap and wiped the sweat from his forehead.

The soft murmur of Globe News could be heard above the chatter of iced coffee drinkers. Hero glanced at the TV on the wall as

flashed across the screen.

Hero stared at the headline with his mouth gaping open. It was one thing giving a name to a heatwave and treating it like a celebrity, but to cancel the most famous football championship – that was going too far.

One of Dad's more interesting encyclopaedic facts was that the World Cup didn't take place in 1942 and 1946 due to the Second World War. Surely the heatwave wasn't as serious as a war? Even if it was bad enough to be called Bertha.

'Come on, let's keep moving,' Dad said, marching off.

In the arrival hall, a scrum of people stood behind a grey metal barrier. Hero leaned forward to see what the commotion was all about.

The crowd parted to show a man and woman from St John Ambulance assisting a plump, red-faced lady who had collapsed into a heap on the floor. **'Heatstroke!'** said Dad. 'It plays havoc with the homeostatic state of the human body.'

Hero frowned. 'What are they doing?'

'Don't tell me you've forgotten what to do in an emergency?' said Dad, raising an eyebrow.

Dad had lectured Hero for months on how to save a life, until he gave in and agreed to learn basic first aid. Hero had endured Dad's endless testing on what to do with a broken bone, a bleeding cut or a maggot-infested wound.

'No, of course not,' said Hero, with a sheepish smile.

It wasn't long before travellers from the seven continents flowed through the sliding doors.

Dad stood gazing into the distance with a two-line frown carved on his brow.

After a while, he scratched his greying hair and said, 'Don't you think this place is a verifiable melting pot of colour, culture and couture?'

Hero rolled his eyes. 'Oh no, please not again,' he muttered.

'Did you know there are forty-three thousand airports in the world?' said Dad.

Hero braced himself.

'The United States has the largest number, with over fourteen thousand,' Dad continued, 'although that's no surprise given the size of the country.'

All the signs were there: the reflective frown, the stare into space and the scratch of the head.

'If we have any chance of stopping global warming and heatwaves like this one, we definitely need to reduce flying,' said Dad.

There was no doubt about it:

Dad had entered Download Knowledge Mode.

Hero would have given anything at that moment to close his ears and block out Dad's endless babble. But, according to Dad, the only members of the animal kingdom blessed with an ear-closing ability were hippos, polar bears and beavers. And the last time he looked in the mirror, he certainly wasn't one of them.

Faced with this undeniable truth, Hero focused his attention on the new batch of jet-setters, which included a young Chinese couple, a group of Italian schoolkids, a sullen businessman and two women in saris.

The stream of passengers eventually came to an end.

Hero and Dad were now the only people left in the hall except for a few glum-looking travellers who had lost their luggage. Hero stared at the sliding doors, which were unwilling to release new arrivals anytime soon.

'She's not coming,' he said, dropping his shoulders in disappointment.

Hero longed for her to return. He couldn't bear to be alone with his factual father a minute longer. But the million-dollar question was when?

'She may be delayed at customs again,' said Dad, rubbing his stubbled chin in thought. 'I hope she hasn't brought anything illegal into the country. You remember that Aztec dagger? She didn't let them take that without a fight.'

'But it's the third time this week she hasn't turned up,' said Hero. 'Can we go now?'

Suddenly, the doors slid open to show a grey-haired,

slim, sun-kissed lady. She wore a yellow, maroon and white patterned kaftan and a chunky red-beaded necklace. A couple of men in uniform accompanied her. The younger of the two pushed a trolley piled up with a battered suitcase and an unusual wrapped object covered in brown crumpled paper and dirty string.

The older man stood at her elbow.

 'GRAN!' yelled Hero.

Gran narrowed her eyes, smiled and tried to lift one arm in the air to wave. It was then Hero saw that Gran was **HANDCUFFED**.

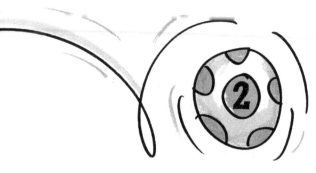

Desperate for a Cuppa

Hero stood dumbfounded as the older man in uniform unlocked the handcuffs.

'You're one of the loveliest criminals I have ever had to arrest,' he said, giving Gran's sunburnt hand a squeaky kiss.

Gran **shuddered** as if an ice cube had just been thrown down her back.

'Oh, Ajay, you're a true officer and a gentleman, and a credit to the Nigerian police force.'

'I'm sorry my country has been so unwelcoming to such a magnificent woman,' said the man. 'I will let you go here. That's the least I can do.'

The officers escorted Gran through the barrier, said their goodbyes and left. Hero bounded forward, wrapping his arms around Gran's skinny body.

'My word, haven't you grown!' Gran said, squeezing Hero close.

Hero sunk himself into Gran's warm embrace. The rough cotton of her kaftan with its exotic aroma of burnt wood and sweet flowers scratched against his face.

'What happened?' he asked, eager to know more. 'Why have you come back so soon?'

'Not now, dear,' said Gran, waving away the questions like flies. 'I'm as parched as a camel's behind and desperate for a cuppa.'

At home, and several cups of tea later, Gran told her latest tale from her motorbiking tour of Africa.

'Well, after leaving Ethel with her new love in the desert, I took myself off to Nigeria. There, I stayed in a delightful village. But I soon found out the villagers were being bullied. And I **HATE bullies**.'

'Bullied?' Hero asked in a soft tone. 'By who?'

'A bloomin' energy company, of all things. They wanted to demolish their homes and drill for gas. Well, I wasn't having any of that. So I started a protest!'

Gran took a gulp of tea from a fine bone-china cup and saucer covered in yellow daffodils.

'**Ahhhh**, that's good,' she said, smacking her lips. 'In the end I had no choice but to chain myself to their machinery!'

Hero was engrossed.

'It took several hours for them to cut me out. Then they threw me into a dingy pit of a cell. The villagers weren't happy – nor was I for that matter. There was uproar! Demonstrations!'

'What happened?' said Hero, leaning forward.

'I'd upset Tyranrox, or is it Tyrones?'

'Who?' said Hero, frowning.

'The energy company. I caused massive disruption to their gas operation. The state governor said I was a national security threat, and he insisted on sending me home.'

'Really?' said Hero, surprised that Gran could ever be a threat. That was for maniacs with bombs in their underpants, not his gran. **NO WAY!**

'That governor was in cahoots with those energy people – it's clear as the lines on my face,' said Gran, taking another gulp of tea.

Later that afternoon, Dad was back in his study, working on his project to update Cuthbert's encyclopaedia collection. Gran unpacked her African souvenirs and put them on the sideboard. They included carved ebony figures, objects made from swamp grass and palm leaves, and a wooden bowl filled with semi-precious coloured gemstones. She then placed in the corner of the living room a large rosewood statue of a tribesman covered in shells and coral beads, bearing a spear.

'You've been doing well since I've been away,' she said, admiring Hero's football trophies and medals on the top shelf. 'When did you get this one?' She picked up a glistening silver cup, which was the only thing not coated in dust.

'I won Footballer of the Year at school last week …' said Hero, his voice petering out.

'How wonderful!' beamed Gran. 'I bet your dad was proud to see you pick this up.'

Hero scowled. 'He wasn't there. He was too busy putting up the shelves for Cuthbert's encyclopaedias.'

'Your father and **those books**!' said Gran with a disapproving nod. 'I thought he might find more time for you while I was away.'

Hero lowered his head and stared at the grain in the wooden floorboards. If anything, Dad had got worse in the nine months Gran had been motorbiking around Africa.

Gran stroked Hero's mousy brown hair. 'I was thinking about you on the plane,' she said in a soothing voice. 'I was reading all about the World Cup. It's only a few weeks away now. Is your dad going to take you?'

'I don't know,' said Hero with a shrug.

'I'll ask him. He's had enough time to sort himself out.'

'**NO!**' snapped Hero.

Despite giving Dad an article from *Goal!* magazine about how to get tickets months earlier, Hero still didn't know whether Dad had bought any. He wanted to ask but Dad was always busy with his project, and Hero never got around to it. Anyway, Dad should have remembered. After all, he'd promised.

'I'll do it,' lied Hero.

Be the Change

That night it was too hot to sleep, despite having the window wide open. Hero lay on top of his bed in his pyjamas, holding a photo of Mum in his hand. It had been two years since she had died, but he still felt a numbing emptiness inside as if it were yesterday. He took a deep breath and stared at the picture. Things would have been so different if Mum were alive. He closed his eyes, trying to remember her cheery smile and warm hugs. He imagined hearing Mum's soft voice like a distant, indistinguishable echo.

'Well done, my darling,' it said. 'I'm so proud of you.'

Hero gave a heavy **Sigh** that turned into a sniffle.

'Oh, Mum, what should I do about Dad?'

Mum believed if people were unhappy, they should do something about it. She had always stood up and spoken out while others complained. She had tried to stop Leaford Council, where Dad worked as an accountant, from selling the school playing fields to a supermarket chain, and the old Art Deco cinema being turned into a nightclub. Her favourite motto from the Indian activist, Ghandi, was

'BE THE CHANGE YOU WANT TO SEE.'

Hero whispered the words to himself, wondering if he could ever get Dad to change.

'Night-night, Mum,' he said, kissing the photo. He carefully placed it on the bedside cabinet and switched off his football lamp. He then snuggled into the pillow, thinking about being the change he wanted to see until he fell into a deep slumber.

The next day something niggled Hero like an itch that had to be scratched. The World Cup was now only weeks away. He dreamed of seeing Leaford City's star striker, Waggie, play in the football championship. It had kept him going over the last two years – a flicker of colour in his grey life. Not only that, if he could just get Dad to put down Cuthbert's books, then maybe he'd be the father he used to know.

After Mum passed away, Dad spent most days sitting on the sofa staring at the wall. Then one day a large box arrived containing twenty-eight encyclopaedias and a pile of tatty files filled with handwritten notes. Dad had inherited the collection from his old friend Mr Cuthbert, an author and the chief librarian at Leaford Library. Overnight Dad had a new purpose in life – to update *Cuthbert's Encyclopaedia of World Knowledge*.

Bound by his task, Dad browsed bookshops in his lunch hour and brought home all sorts of books for his research. It wasn't long before they took over the house – on the stairs, down the side of the sofa, on top of the fridge, in every nook and cranny. Dad no longer wanted to see Leaford City play, watch TV, visit his allotment or go to the cinema. Dad had become

BORING.

It was then that Hero joined Leaford Primary's football team, where he discovered he could dance through a defence, play a perfect one-two and score a goal. The school won the Leafordshire League for the first time in over twenty years, winning every single match. Dad may have had his books, but Hero had his football.

Hero entered Dad's study. It was a pokey room **crammed** with an overflowing mahogany bookcase, a faded antique bureau and a threadbare brown-leather armchair. It had become Dad's hideaway, the place where he assimilated facts about nature, science, humanities and the arts.

He scanned the room, determined to find the World Cup article he had given Dad. In the corner, two newly assembled shelves, laden with thick volumes of Cuthbert's encyclopaedias, hung on the wall above the old armchair.

Hero searched beside the chair but there was nothing, so he tried underneath. Catching the sight of a crumpled ball of coloured paper, he squeezed behind the back of the chair, bent down and grabbed it.

Hero raised his head, hitting the shelf.

As he moved away, two screws fell from the hinges. Hero picked them up and placed them back into the holes that were now too big. He gave a sarcastic sniff. Dad was useless at DIY.

He pushed the chair against the wall and unravelled the ball of paper. It was the article from *Goal!* magazine.

His heart twinged with disappointment. It was clear Dad had forgotten about his promise and thrown the page away. A ripple of anger spread through Hero's body, like the sun burning from inside. He needed to get out.

Dad Problem

There was a stillness in the air that morning so fragile it could break at any moment. Hero stood in the back garden feeling the feathery ripples of heat tickle his nostrils. He stared at his tatty football, imagining he was in a World Cup penalty shoot-out.

It was the last chance for him to win the game. Keeping his cool, he hurtled towards the ball, kicking it hard. The ball flew into the air and hit the side of the sycamore tree, gliding across the bone-dry garden and bouncing off the dilapidated shed before smashing against the fence.

He had done it.

'YEAH!'

He had scored the winning goal, and for a split second, joy eclipsed his sadness.

Suddenly, there was a clang of metal bolts and the click of locks as his neighbour's well-secured kitchen door opened.

Not in the mood to be interrogated by his nosy neighbour, Hero fled into Borromeo Road.

There, he walked along the beech-lined avenue of red-brick houses. Scorched yellow patches had replaced the pea-green gardens, and the once gleaming cars now stood dusty on the drive. Heatwave Blistering Bertha was affecting the whole country – with drought, hosepipe bans and heatstroke.

Eventually, Hero came to the brown metal gate of his friend Mitzy's house. To his surprise, the gate opened, revealing a line of silver, mushroom-shaped light sensors. He walked down the stone path, but before he reached the front door, a tall girl with short auburn hair, square glasses and skin the colour of cinnamon appeared.

'You took your time,' she said sharply.

'I've been busy,' Hero replied.

'You'd better come in before you fry.'

Hero entered the darkened living room, which was illuminated by little red and green lights dispersed here and there.

'Drink this before you dehydrate,' said Mitzy. She thrust a welcome glass of cool water into his hand. Hero gulped it down.

'Have you noticed the new additions to the house?' asked Mitzy. 'It is part of my plan to have the smartest home in the country. What do you think?'

She stared at him, her eyes demanding a response.

'Err … it's great,' replied Hero, not sure what to make of it.

'Leia ensures the living room maintains a comfortable temperature,' she said.

'Leia?'

Mitzy straightened her hair and purred, 'My voice-activated assistant!'

'Oh,' said Hero, confused. 'Err … what do your parents say?' he said, trying to hide his ignorance.

'Mum is super keen, but Dad … well … he just complains. He's such a **technophobe**!'

Suddenly, a robotic voice said, 'Excuse me, you have a guest waiting outside.'

A grainy monochrome picture of Partha at the gate

appeared on a small screen.

'Our infrared surveillance system can detect any intruder, even next door's tortoise when it escapes!' said Mitzy. She flashed a smug smile at Hero. 'Leia, allow my guest entry.'

It wasn't long before Partha was in the lounge, yawning and scratching his cropped black hair as Mitzy boasted about her technology-enhanced house.

When she stopped, Partha looked at Hero. 'What's wrong with you? You've just won Footballer of the Year, your gran is back from her travels and you're going to the big school in September. You should be happy.'

Hero said nothing and gazed at the flashing amber bars of a monitor on the sideboard.

'Come on, tell us what's on your mind,' insisted Mitzy. 'Problems are like bags of shopping: it's easy to carry them when you share the load.'

Hero took a deep breath. It was pointless trying to resist Mitzy – she always got her own way, ever since pre-school.

'It's Dad,' he said in a timid voice. 'He spends all his time filling his head with stupid facts.'

'I know he's a bore, but he ain't that bad,' said Partha. 'He told me that "uncopyrightable" is the longest word in the English language that can be spelled without repeating any letters. My Auntie Fatima was dead impressed when I told her.'

'But he's scaring people away,' protested Hero. 'The neighbours cross the road rather than pass our house. Even the postman leaves our mail next door to avoid coming up the path. It's got to stop!'

'Look on the bright side: at least your dad ain't a walking stink bomb.'

'What?' frowned Hero.

'I nearly died when Dad **dropped one** in front of Roxburgh at parents' evening. They're always silent and deadly, especially after dhal curry,' said Partha, rolling his eyes.

'My dad is useless with technology,' chimed in Mitzy. 'He can't send a text, use the remote or set his watch, and he shouts at Leia as if she's a dog.'

'Why are you telling me this?' complained Hero.

'Cos you ain't the only one who has to put up with an **EMBARRASSING DAD**!' said Partha.

Juice of Life

Hero didn't know whether he felt better or worse after talking to his friends when he returned home for lunch. Having a dad who stinks is nothing compared to one who's always got a book in front of his face. As for Mitzy, she's such a techno-geek she couldn't understand anyone who might not be the same.

Hero plonked himself down at the pine kitchen table, where he eyed an unusual conical brown clay pot surrounded by red, blue and yellow wicker place mats.

'There you go!' Gran said, taking off the lid. 'Moroccan tagine complete with the exotic spices of cumin, turmeric, cinnamon, saffron and paprika.'

Hero **wrinkled** his nose at the peculiar aroma of lamb, prune and almond stew that wafted down the table.

'Mustapha from Morocco taught me how to make this,' said Gran proudly. 'He believes if you're hot on the inside, you're cooler on the outside. And we certainly need cooling down in this heat!'

'Can't we have fish fingers and chips instead?' pleaded Hero.

'Son, we have over **ten thousand taste buds**,' said Dad with a frown. 'Evolution would not have endowed us with the ability to enjoy sweet, bitter, salty, sour and spicy if all we ate was fish fingers and chips.'

Hero gave a disappointed stare at the stew and couscous piled on his plate. Evolution had a lot to answer for, not enabling people to close their ears or eat fish fingers and chips every day.

'Come on, **BE ADVENTUROUS**!' said Gran, beaming. 'Mustapha calls this the juice of life!'

Dad took a mouthful of stew, then gave a heavy cough before sipping some water.

'Have you seen my new shelves, Mother?' he said, clearing his throat. 'Mr Cuthbert's encyclopaedia collection finally has a home.'

'I don't know why you bother with those books,' Gran huffed. 'They're just gathering dust. And as for those shelves you've put up, they're more unhinged than old Beryl Banner. You need to get rid of the lot of them!'

'I'm honoured to maintain Mr Cuthbert's literary legacy,' protested Dad. 'I can't let him down.'

Hero stared at his plate, playing with the prunes with his spoon.

'And you should stop bothering the neighbours with your factuality,' said Gran, giving Dad another dollop of stew. 'First Beryl Banner and now poor Mr Percy. When will it all end?'

'Mr Percy was complaining the weather had gone all topsy-turvy. I explained to him the hockey-stick graph of global temperatures. I was saying …'

Hero yawned and slouched further into his chair as Dad once again bombarded them with bullets of knowledge: **'climate change'**, **'greenhouse effect'**, **'ice caps melting'** …

After lunch, Dad retreated to his book den to finish an encyclopaedic entry on human ecology. Gran arranged her African holiday snaps in the conservatory. Hero lay on the living-room sofa with the curtains drawn and a fan blasting away. Mum's words played in his head like a stuck CD:

'BE THE CHANGE YOU WANT TO SEE.'

He stared at the TV, ignoring the adverts that flashed across the screen in the dim light. Until one asked,

'ARE YOU WORLD CUP READY?
Enjoy the splendour, excitement and thrill of the world's **GREATEST** championship in high-definition Technicolour ...'

The advert showed a man and woman sitting on a sofa next to two kids watching footie on a large TV. They jumped up, cheering and punching the air when a team scored a goal.

Hero squirmed at the sight of it, for he used to do the same with Mum and Dad. But those days were now long gone. He would give anything to watch football as a family again and stop Dad from hiding behind his encyclopaedias.

'Be the change you want to see?' he muttered to himself with a sarcastic tone.

If Dad couldn't be bothered, then why should he?

He flung his head back on the cushion in anger.

Ouch! It was hard.

He looked underneath it to find one of Dad's old hardback books by Diego de Valera, called *Treatise on Arms*.

He **threw** it across the room.

And it was at that precise moment the ground

TREMBLED.

The walls **SWAYED**.

The windows **RATTLED**.

The floor **CREAKED**.

The books **SHUDDERED**.

The ornaments **DANCED**.

The **SWAYING** got FASTER ...

and ... FASTER ...

until

the

whole

house

SHOOK.

Old Buffalo

Hero jumped up and stared at the wall. It was as if a herd of elephants were tap dancing down Borromeo Road.

The shaking then stopped as abruptly as it had started. A curious stillness descended on the house only to be broken by one almighty

CRAAASSSSSSH!

Hero ran to Dad's study and peered round the door.

Dad's new shelves had collapsed, and a pile of thick leather-bound volumes of *Cuthbert's Encyclopaedia of World Knowledge* now covered the armchair.

Hero stood rooted to the spot, staring at the scrawny, hairy, snow-white legs and Union flag flip-flops sticking out from under the encyclopaedias.

'He's been killed by knowledge!' shrieked Gran, appearing at the door. 'I told him all those facts and figures would be the end of him.'

Hero glanced at the mountain of books.

'Oh noooo!' A sickening guilt weighed down on him at the thought that hitting his head on the shelves might have dislodged them.

With his heart twanging like an elastic band, he rushed to the chair and flung aside the encyclopaedias volume by volume to reveal a skinny, lifeless body.

'Check if he's breathing,' said Gran, her voice cracking with despair.

Hero grabbed Dad by the arms and shook him as hard as he could.

Dad remained still.

'DAD!' he yelled, shaking him again.

Dad moved his head and groaned.

'ARRRrrrrrr.'

'Thank goodness!' said Gran with her hands on her cheeks. 'I'll phone for an ambulance.'

Whey-faced and helpless, Dad now lay slumped in the chair, his knowledge-searching brain dormant. Hero and Gran placed an ice pack on his brow, a cushion behind his neck and put his legs on a stool. They left him in the study to prepare a bag for the hospital.

When they returned, Dad was on his feet looking at a picture on the wall he had bought from a car boot sale many years ago. It was of a woman surrounded by a colourful aura of red, orange, yellow, blue, indigo and violet. She had sorrowful eyes and a single tear on her cheek. The lady wore a flowing green gown made of leaves. In her hands she held a large darkened spherical object that resembled a dying Earth.

'Dad, are you okay?' asked Hero, sensing something was not right.

Dad continued to stare at the picture, his face changed.

'What are you looking at?' Hero asked.

'My mother,' whispered Dad in an unusual, deep voice.

Hero scowled.

'I'm your mother,' squeaked Gran. 'You're Eddie

Trough, and for the record your father was Derek Trough.'

Dad winced and touched the side of his head. 'I need water. I have thirst. I need food. I have hunger.'

'You've just had your lunch,' said Hero, confused.

Dad screwed up his face and glared at Hero.

'Come on, I'll get you tea and toast,' said Gran. 'I always find T and T useful in a crisis. We could have done with some after we escaped the raging rhinos crossing the Serengeti.'

Hero helped Dad into the living room and sat him on the sofa. After a few minutes, Gran returned with a mug of tea and two slices of toast. Dad took a gulp of tea and spat it out.

'What is this?' he said in disgust.

Hero ran to the kitchen and brought back a glass of water. Dad poured the drink down his throat with great satisfaction. He then tore off a piece of soggy toasted white bread as if it were a strip of meat and ate it.

'Why don't you have a rest?' suggested Gran. 'I'm sure you'll feel much better for it.'

'The body is weary as an old buffalo,' replied Dad, his eyelids flickering. 'I need to sleep so I can awake reborn like the rising sun.'

With that, he finished his water and toast, closed his eyes and lay on the sofa with a serene smile.

Hero's chest tightened.

Old buffalo?
Rising sun?

Why was Dad acting so weird?

Earth Warrior

'**This heat!** It's worse than the Sahara,' said Gran, pacing up and down, the lines on her face deepening. 'Did I tell you about our tyres melting in the desert?'

Although Gran's tales were more interesting than Dad's boring facts, there was a time and place for everything, and this was definitely not the time.

'We had run out of water. Vultures were circling. We were sure it was the end,' said Gran, gazing into space. 'Then, out of the blue, a nomadic tribe arrived. They took us in, treated us like their own. They were so nice, Ethel ended up marrying the chief. I do—'

KNOCK, KNOCK, KNOCK!

'They're here!' yelled Hero, rushing to the front door.

It wasn't long before a rather jovial paramedic wearing a luminous polo shirt and shorts was taking notes.

Hero recalled what Dad had said.

'Old buffalo! There's not many roaming around in these parts,' chortled the paramedic.

'Now then, let's see the damage.' He lifted Dad's eyelids and shone a bright light into his eyes. 'Eddie, can you hear me?' he yelled. 'You've been knocked out by knowledge.'

There was no response. Dad lay still and silent.

The paramedic then pulled out a stethoscope from his shoulder bag, listened to Dad's chest and took his pulse. 'In these situations, we usually get some reaction. You know, the lights are on but nobody's at home – but it looks as if he's gone and moved house altogether!' he said.

'What can we do?' asked Hero, concerned Dad might never come round.

'Now don't you worry, sonny Jim. I've my own tried and tested method for such eventualities,' grinned the paramedic.

'What?' Hero asked.

'The chief medical officer won't like it, but what do the high and mighty know about the practicalities of the job, eh?'

The paramedic grabbed the end of Dad's nose between his two fingers and gave it a hard twist. Dad sprung to life and let out a loud

'My twist and shout technique,' laughed the paramedic. 'Gets them every time!'

Hero sucked in a breath. The paramedic's approach was unusual, but at least Dad was awake.

'Now we've got your attention,' said the paramedic, 'let's do a reality check.'

Dad stared at the floor, his blue eyes frozen.

'Come on, Dad, say something,' whispered Hero.

'Eddie, what is your name?' asked the paramedic.

Hero squeezed his lips together. What a stupid question.

'Oh, that was a giveaway,' sniggered the paramedic.

Dad remained silent.

'I'll ask again. What's your name?'

Silence.

'Strange,' said the paramedic, scratching his head.

'Come on, I'll give you a clue,' said Gran, looking on. 'It begins with E.'

Nothing.

'Let me have a go,' said Hero.

He moved closer to Dad and tried to smile but couldn't quite manage it.

'Dad, you can do it,' he whispered. 'What are you called?'

Dad blinked several times, as if he had been switched on. He turned to Hero, and in a deep, firm voice, which was so different from his normal tone, he said, 'I … am … Terra … Firma.'

'Terry who?' exclaimed Hero, not believing his ears.

'A …
warrior …
of …
the …
Earth.'

Leaford General

A heavy aroma of body odour and disinfectant hung in the air at Leaford General's crowded Accident and Emergency department. It was the next morning, and Dad had been kept in overnight for observation on a trolley in A & E due to a shortage of beds.

'How much longer?' asked Hero, fanning himself with his baseball cap.

'Patience! The staff are overworked,' said Gran with a knowing look. 'The doctor is giving your father a full service, just like when my motorbike goes in for an MOT. That reminds me. I must see the Harley Gals; they're desperate to hear about Ethel and her new husband.'

Hero scanned the waiting room. It resembled

a traffic-light conference, crowded with sunburnt individuals beaming red.

'But Dad's an accountant,' Hero said. 'How can he think he's a warrior called Terry?'

'Mother Earth, buffalos, warriors – it's all **baloney**! The doctors will sort him out, just you wait and see,' said Gran.

She made one of her 'don't worry, everything's going to be fine' faces. But what if Dad never got better? After all, he wouldn't be the first member of the Trough family to have gone bonkers. Mum had always said Great Uncle Dave was doolally after he turned to hugging trees and tried to marry an old oak.

As for Gran … well …

Hero chewed his lip, thinking what he could do. At that moment, a workman in a dirty white vest with beetroot-coloured shoulders increased the volume of the flat-screen TV on the wall. The voice of Globe News blared across the waiting room.

'The Geological Survey has confirmed that an earthquake hit Leafordshire yesterday,' said the silver-haired newsreader, Alistair Homes. 'The 4.9 magnitude tremors centred on the city of Leaford. No damage or injuries have been reported. Now, over to our award-winning roving reporter, Robin Rivett,' said Homes.

Rivett was a short man with an eyepatch, greased-back black hair and a thick charcoal beard.

'Leaford is breaking all records,' he said. 'Not only is it the hottest place in the country, it has just experienced its first earthquake. I have with me Chief Councillor Erik Onions, who is the head of the council and responsible for the civil emergency response.'

An elephantine figure in a navy-blue suit with several chins overflowing from his tight white shirt-collar gave a serious grin.

'What are you doing to help the people of Leaford in this time of natural disasters?' asked Rivett with a microphone in his hand.

'Ahem … well … the earthquake has caused no major casualties,' said Onions, tilting his head as if to show off his good side. 'Regarding Heatwave Blistering Bertha, we've informed the whole community to wear bathing costumes, drink lots of water so they pee at least four times a day, draw their curtains and stay cool.'

Onions wiped droplets of sweat from his orange pumpkin face with a polka-dot handkerchief.

'We will carry on providing an efficient service, even

under such extreme conditions,' he said with a grin.

'EARTHQUAKES?

In Leaford?' gasped Hero, his eyes widening. He never imagined they were possible in Leafordshire.

'Things like this are here to challenge us,' said Gran, unsurprised. 'I told Ethel the same thing when we got lost in the tombs of Aksum.'

'What?' said Hero with a puzzled glare.

'The lights had failed; we were left in pitch blackness, lost in a labyrinth of underground corridors. The air was getting thinner and thinner. It was like having a hangman's noose round one's neck. Ethel was on the verge of having one of her funny turns, then—'

'I'm very sorry,' interrupted the nurse. 'Mr Trough seems to have disappeared.'

'What?' said Hero, scowling. 'We came here to get him back, not lose him!'

'You'd better come with me,' said the nurse, looking utterly miserable.

Hero and Gran followed the nurse down a corridor of green-curtained cubicles. At the end, she stopped and opened a curtain. 'The last time we saw him, he was lying on the trolley here.'

Hero's eyes swept the cubicle like a metal detector. 'He's left all his clothes!' he said, pointing to the chair.

'Love a duck!' said Gran, crumpling up her face. 'Don't tell me your father's gone *au naturel*?'

Hero ran off and searched every cubicle, cringing at the idea of Dad walking around the hospital **NAKED**.

After being told off by the sister for disturbing the patients, Hero returned to the waiting room, where he found onlookers bemused by a tall, slim, mushroom-white figure standing at reception, wearing nothing but his black briefs. Hero took in a deep breath ready to shout across the crowded A & E but thought better of it. Instead, he hurried towards Dad.

'Come on, Dad, err … Terra Firma,' said Hero, pulling Dad away from the counter.

'Who is that man?' said Dad, glancing back at the receptionist, who stared open-mouthed.

'He works for the NHS,' said Hero, leading Dad back to the cubicle.

'NHS tribe?' said Dad, bemused.

A Car-riage Awaits

Hero persuaded Dad to put on his clothes. After some time, a curly-haired doctor wearing a white coat arrived to give his diagnosis.

'Mr Trough has traumatic concussion,' declared Dr Anagnostopoulos, fidgeting with pens overflowing from his breast pocket.

'When will he get better?' asked Hero eagerly.

'Good question! Some people are back to normal after a couple of days, others … well … they can take months … even years. We just don't know.'

Hero gave an incredulous gasp. '**Years?**'

'Your dad has golf-ball-sized bumps all over his head,' said Dr Anagnostopoulos, twirling his hand above his wiry hair. 'They have affected parts of the brain that deal with memory and imagination. That is why he may not be himself.'

'But he says he's a warrior and that the Earth is his mother,' said Hero, leaning forward.

'A what?' said the doctor, befuddled.

'Some kind of earth warrior.'

'Did your father have any connection with green groups before the incident?' asked the medic, chewing the end of a pencil.

'No, not really,' said Hero.

'Has he been watching any environmental documentaries?'

'No, he doesn't like TV any more.'

'Does he know any eco-activists?' suggested Dr Anagnostopoulos.

'The only person he knows is Compost Jack,' Hero replied. 'He helped Dad set up his composting bin. He's well known in Leaford for having the lowest carbon footprint in the country.'

'Don't forget that Mo at Edible Leaford,' added Gran. 'Is he still going around planting his veggies on the verges?' she said with dreamy eyes. 'He was such a nice man. He had a lovely smile and ooh … that twinkle in his eye could dazzle any girl's heart.'

Hero shook his head, exasperated.

'Hmmm, a very unusual case,' said the doctor, chewing harder on the pencil.

'There's an ecological picture in his study,' said Hero, remembering the car boot buy.

'A static visual image would have had a minimal effect,' said Dr Anagnostopoulos. 'Perhaps it's Heatwave Blistering Bertha? She's turning lots of people loopy.'

The doctor bit the pencil, causing it to break. He spat out the splinters and coughed several times.

'Well … whatever has caused Mr Trough to think he's an earth warrior, the treatment is the same.'

'What's that?' asked Hero.

'Patience! It may seem strange, but you need to go along with his world,' said the doctor.

'You mean I've got to pretend Dad is an earth warrior?' barked Hero, trying to compute what he had just heard.

'If that is how he's behaving, I'm afraid so. Why don't you consider him a foreign guest, if it helps you?'

'Can't we do anything to get him back?' pleaded Hero. 'What about hitting him on the head again?'

'That only happens in the movies,' laughed Dr Anagnostopoulos. 'In fact, that's the last thing your father needs. Another hit to the head could have long-term irreparable consequences.'

'Are you sure there's nothing we can do for him?' said Gran with a look of despair.

'He must recover naturally. We will just have to wait and see how this condition manifests itself.'

Hero and Gran exchanged a wide-eyed glance.

'He can go home with you now, but he needs total rest,' said the doctor.

'If he deteriorates, bring him back. Otherwise, I'll see him at my clinic for a follow-up appointment.'

A short while later, Hero and Gran **frogmarched** Dad across the hospital car park. The summer holidays were not going the way Hero had hoped. He should be playing footie with his mates, not hanging around crowded airports and smelly hospitals.

Gran sighed. 'Life is subject to change without notice. That's what Ethel always says. She's right! I said it's unhealthy for a man his age to be cooped up with all that knowledge. It could affect his mind.'

'It's too late,' muttered Hero.

Gran frowned caringly at Hero. 'Are you okay,

dear?' she said. 'You've got a face as white as the cliffs of Dover.'

'I can't believe Dad thinks he's an earth warrior,' groaned Hero. 'It's just super weird.'

Gran placed a reassuring hand on Hero's shoulder and gazed at him with her dark chestnut eyes.

'I know it hasn't been easy for you and your dad these last few years,' said Gran. 'What with your mum going and your dad developing his obsession with Cuthbert's books.'

She paused before twitching a thin smile. 'I guess my gallivanting hasn't helped. But I'm here now, and we will get things back on track.'

Hero gave a lacklustre nod before stopping in front of Gran's yellow Ford Fiesta.

Dad stared at the metal machine. 'What is this?' he asked, tilting his head.

'It's a car,' answered Hero.

'A car?'

'Yes, it's like, err …'

Hero hesitated, trying to find words to explain.

'It's a car-riage. It will transport you home.'

Dad studied the car with naive curiosity. 'Has the medicine man given this thing to me?' he asked. 'Where are the horses?'

Hero glanced at Gran through the windscreen, wondering what to say.

'They are inside here,' he said, pointing to the front of the car.

Dad moved closer to the vehicle, pausing before placing his ear to the bonnet.

went the engine.

Dad jumped back, startled by the noise.

'The medicine man has put fierce beasts in there!' exclaimed Dad.

'Come on, get in!' yelled Gran. 'You'll feel much better after some of my South African roasted chicken and a bean salad!'

Earth Prophecy

A warm breeze blasted through the car window, ruffling Hero's hair. Gran leaned against the steering wheel, gripping it tightly, squinting at the road ahead. Dad sat stiff and silent.

The car crossed a roundabout, flinging Hero and Dad to the side.

Then **SCREeeech!**

went the vehicle at the bend as Gran drove as if she were on her motorbike.

Hero and Dad were flung across the backseat. Dad's eyes bulged from their sockets.

Hero stared at the muddled colours of pedestrians whooshing by as they sped through Leaford city centre. Pretending that Dad was a warrior would not be easy.

How was he going to explain it to Mitzy and Partha? Worst of all, what if their nosy neighbour, Mr Bugwell, found out? The whole of Borromeo Road would know then.

The car **jerked** to a halt, **hurling** Hero and Dad forward.

A group of cherry-faced individuals in shorts, T-shirts and hats, thrusting placards in the air, marched across the road followed by an older lady on a metallic-pink mobility scooter.

'What's going on here?' said Gran, narrowing her eyes.

'It's that Chief Councillor Onions – he sold the school playing fields and now the Rec,' said Hero, leaning forward to get a better view. 'We've got nowhere to play footie now.'

'ONCE YOU FRACK, YOU CAN'T GO BACK! NO FRACKING IN LEAFORD!'

yelled the protestors.

'Eddie, what's this fracking? It sounds like a bad word,' Gran said, glancing at Dad.

Dad said nothing, his face pallid and expressionless.

Gran gave a quick glance over her shoulder. 'Oh, this business will take some getting used to.'

'They pump water and chemicals into the ground,' said Hero proudly.

'What?' Gran frowned.

'Fracking! Dad told me about it,' said Hero. 'The earth cracks and releases gas. It would be much better to invest in solar and wind energy – at least then we'll have somewhere to play footie.'

'First in Nigeria and now here.' Gran sighed. 'Where will it all end?'

It wasn't long before they arrived at number 32 Borromeo Road.

'Come on, you need a rest before tea,' said Gran.

Hero took Dad by the arm and guided him up the path and into the house.

Inside, Dad studied with interest Gran's collection of African souvenirs. 'Our brothers and sisters may live in different lands,' said Dad, inspecting a carved ebony figure in his hand. 'But we are all children of Mother Earth.'

Hero winced. Sooner or later the neighbours would notice Dad going all **ECO-HIPPY**. Especially when he no longer drowned them with his new-found knowledge. On the upside, the postman might find the courage to deliver the letters to their house again.

'Why don't you go and see your friends?' said Gran, entering the living room. 'I'll keep an eye on your father.'

Hero went to sit on the hall stairs and sent a text to Mitzy and Partha. Sunrays sparkled through the frosted glass of the front door, turning speckles of dust into glitter. As he followed the sun-glitter gliding effortlessly through the air, images of how things used to be when Mum was alive appeared in his mind like a movie …

KNOCK, KNOCK, KNOCK!

Hero stirred from his deep thought, got up and opened the door to find Mitzy and Partha standing in the sunshine.

'Did you feel the earthquake?' asked Partha, marching in.

'You bet I did!' replied Hero. 'The bookshelf fell off the wall.'

'My Auntie Fatima thinks it's the end of the world: first Blistering Bertha and now Rocking Rafat. She won't stop kissing me goodbye.'

'Rocking Rafat?' exclaimed Hero.

'That's what she calls the earthquake.'

'Your auntie has an overactive imagination,' sneered Mitzy. 'It's only a 4.9 magnitude tremor; I got an alert on my news app.'

'It shattered the glass coffee table,' protested Partha. 'That's a real bad sign.'

'What's up with your dad?' said Mitzy briskly, turning her gaze to Hero.

'It's serious. Come and see,' replied Hero, leading them to the study.

All three entered Dad's knowledge cave. The bookshelves *hung off the wall*,

and the pile of worn leather-bound encyclopaedias lay on the floor.

'All those hit him on the head except that one,' said Hero, pointing to a solitary book clinging to the dislodged shelf. 'Because of that, he's lost his memory and thinks he's some kind of warrior.'

'A warrior?' exclaimed Mitzy and Partha in unison.

'Yeah, it's something to do with Mother Earth,' said Hero in a timid voice.

Mitzy frowned and adjusted her glasses. 'An earth warrior?'

'How did you know?'

'Have you read what's on that picture over there?' said Mitzy, pointing across the room.

Hero moved towards the portrait of the green lady with her haunting dark eyes. Although he had seen the image a **zillion** times, he had never bothered to look at the ornate writing in a faded yellow scroll at the bottom of the picture.

The Earth Prophecy

There will come a time when the Earth will be plundered and polluted. The air will turn grey, the water black and the soil red. Birds will cease to sing, fish to swim, beasts to roam. Humankind will be endangered. On that day, the earth warrior will rise to unite people of all colours, to take over and protect their nature mother.

'That's where he got it from,' gasped Hero, his cheeks growing hot.

'Boys!' Mitzy scolded. She walked over to a pile of encyclopaedias on the floor and thumbed the faded yellow pages. 'Why would anyone want to read such tatty old things, anyway?' she said. 'The internet has everything you need to know.'

'Dad inherited them from Mr Cuthbert at Leaford Library. He wrote them,' said Hero.

'How long did that take?' said Partha, staring at the pile of books.

'Most of his life. He finished his last entry and then dropped dead.'

Mitzy threw her head back and laughed. 'I bet he overloaded his hard drive.'

'He was ninety-nine years old,' said Hero.

'Imagine spending all your time writing this stuff. I'd be bored after the first page.'

'It was his dream to be a scholar of knowledge,' explained Hero. 'Dad says he had a great mind and that his work is exceptional.'

'A health hazard!' said Mitzy, wrinkling her nose. 'They smell like cat's pee.'

'Well, Mr Cuthbert lived with forty cats,' said Hero, feeling his body tense.

'No wonder they **STINK**!'

'Enough about Mr Cuthbert,' snapped Hero. Mitzy and Partha may have thought Dad's condition was a joke, but to Hero it was real. 'I want Dad to be normal,' he said. 'I can't do anything except wait until he's back to his old self.'

'**RESEARCH!**' declared Mitzy. 'I'll get my tablet and we can search the net. There's bound to be something somewhere that will provide the solution to your problem.'

Hero squeezed his lips tight. 'Yes ... but ... we need to give him time to recover,' he said. 'That's what the doctor said. It's got to be natural. He'll be fine tomorrow.'

'What if he isn't?' said Mitzy, crossing her arms and giving one of her bossy pouts. 'You've got to be prepared,' she said.

At that moment, Gran yelled from the kitchen. '**He's gone AGAIN!**'

Extreme Fishing

'I told your father to have a siesta,' said Gran.

'I put the chicken in the oven then nodded off myself. When I came round, he had gone.'

Partha peered into the kitchen with a grin on his face. 'He's wearing his birthday suit. I can tell you that for nothing,' he said. 'Cos all his clothes are in the living room.'

'AGAIN!' Gran glanced up to the ceiling and shook her head.

Hero exhaled deeply. 'Why do warriors have to go around naked?'

He hurried to the kitchen door and looked down the long, yellow, parched lawn; both the shed and back garden gate were wide open.

'He's gone onto the field!'

yelled Hero, running to the bottom of the garden.

He passed through the metal gate and across a patch of wasteland that led to a crumbling grey stone bridge. There, he stood shielding his eyes from the bright sunlight with his hand, searching for Dad along the River Leaf.

'Come on, Dad, where are you?' he muttered under his breath.

A few minutes later, Mitzy and Partha appeared.

'If he carries on like this, you'll have to tag him,' said Mitzy. 'Then we could track him on my tablet.'

Sometimes Mitzy's comments were annoyingly unhelpful.

Gran arrived, gasping for air, sweat rolling down her darkened face.

'Is he on the Rec?' she panted.

'They've blocked the entrance,' said Hero. He

glanced at a newly built wooden fence at the other side of the bridge that led to Leaford Recreational Area, known locally as the Rec.

There was a large white sign with red lettering.

KEEP OUT
PRIVATE PROPERTY
ALL TRESPASSERS
WILL BE PROSECUTED

TYRANOX ENERGY

'TYRANOX!' Gran looked as if she had just sniffed a pair of Hero's sweaty football socks.

'Yeah, it sounds like a dinosaur, doesn't it?' smirked Partha.

'They're trouble!' said Gran in disbelief. 'It's the same bloomin' company that was in Nigeria. Now they're here too!'

'I think I've found him,' yelled Mitzy.

Hero went to the edge of the stone bridge and looked down the river. 'There! There!' he said, pointing to a bush with faded dry leaves curled up like Persian slippers.

The bush moved, releasing foliage into the air, allowing them to glimpse something chalk white.

'If it is him, I do hope he's not starkers!' said Gran, wiping away beads of sweat from her brow.

'Dad!' yelled Hero.

There was no response.

After a few seconds, the tall, skinny, pearl-coloured figure of Dad emerged from behind the bush.

'What – is – he – wearing?' gasped Mitzy, emphasising each word.

The colour drained from Hero's face, for Dad was practically naked. All that covered his modesty was a blue and yellow, patterned, triangular-shaped cover the size of a small handkerchief. It hung from his slim waist by a twine-like, spiralled thread.

'That's the Kirdi loincloth. I bought it when I was in Cameroon!' exclaimed Gran. 'I got the kiddie version, as I didn't have much space in my suitcase. I thought it would make a nice wall hanging.'

In his right hand, Dad held a long wooden brush

handle with a sharp kitchen knife tied to the end with green garden string.

Hero cringed at the sight.

'He looks **SOOOOOOO** weird,' scoffed Partha.

'Really! He's not well,' said Mitzy, trying to be charitable.

'**Dad! Dad!**' yelled Hero, eager to catch his attention.

Dad ignored his call and continued to walk along the riverbank.

'TERRA FIRMA!' shouted Gran.

Dad looked up. Gran smiled and beckoned him to the bridge.

'You'd better stay behind me,' said Gran in a warning voice.

'Why?' asked Hero, scowling at the idea.

'Because that loincloth is the one-piece version – it hasn't got a back cover!'

Hero, Mitzy and Partha hurried to stand behind Gran as Dad sauntered towards them.

'I have hunger. I brought fish from the river that Mother Earth has provided for us,' said Dad, holding up two dead fish.

Hero grimaced at the sight of blood dripping from their bodies. That's all he needed: a half-naked, brush-handled warrior fisherman as a father.

'Very good, now let's go before anyone else sees us,' said Gran with a quick glance around the Rec.

They all hurried home with Hero and his friends striding ahead. As they approached the back gate, Gran turned to Hero. 'I think that's enough excitement for today.'

She had one of her 'don't mess with me' faces on – Hero knew what to do.

'I'll see you tomorrow, guys,' he said.

'Tomorrow?' said Mitzy, shooting a surprised glance at Hero.

Hero stared at her and arched an eyebrow.

'I guess it's time to go then,' she said with a tone of objection. 'I'll try to do more research tonight. Come on, Partha!'

Hero, Gran and Dad returned to an intense burning smell in the kitchen.

'**NO!** My South African-style roast!' cried Gran, flinging her arms in the air. She rushed to switch off the oven, then grabbed her oven gloves and took out a chicken engulfed in flames.

Hero threw a cup of water over the blazing bird.

It **hissed** and **sizzled** as it emitted a mass of grey, choking smoke.

'Fire Bird!' exclaimed Dad. 'Elder, I will call you Fire Bird.'

Hero waved away the mist with a puzzled look. What was he talking about now?

'Because you are fiery as this bird,' said Dad, pointing to the water-sodden black remains of the chicken.

'Oh ... I see ... Fire Bird?' smiled Gran. 'Very nice ... the Kpelle tribe of Liberia used to call me Mamawa Wonlay. It means "tired mother". I must have looked dreadful when they rescued Ethel and me from the river. Our canoe was sinking fast. Then Ethel spotted the legendary Gbahali, a voracious river monster – a cross between a crocodile and a hairless pony. Anyway, it was getting closer and closer. I told Ethel—'

'You, I shall call **Little Shadow**,' said Dad, gazing at Hero. 'Because you follow me like my shadow.'

Hero smiled. He liked the sound of that. At least it was better than some of the nicknames he had been called at school.

'Now I must nourish the body,' said Dad, holding up the blood-covered fish.

64

Hero glanced at Gran in desperation, wondering what Dad was going to do next.

Later that afternoon, Dad made a fire in the back garden from the dried-up branches of a dead tree. Gran put up a green and white gazebo to shade them from the sun. It was odd lighting a fire in a heatwave, but Hero was no longer surprised at Dad's **WEIRD WARRIOR BEHAVIOUR**. Dad chopped off the heads of the fish and removed their bloody insides before cooking their remains. Hero flinched at the sight.

'Delicious,' said Gran with a hoarse voice, after choking on a fish bone.

Hero preferred fish fingers.

'We've got to cover up your father,' said Gran, staring at Dad's skinny body. 'I don't know what the neighbours will think if they see him wearing a Kirdi kiddie's one-piece.'

'He won't wear clothes,' said Hero, wishing Dad would. 'He says he wants to feel the energy of Mother Earth.'

'Wait! I've an idea,' she said, hurrying off into the house.

A little while later, Gran returned holding up two large mustard chamois-leather window cloths that she had sewn together. Dad smiled and stood up to put on the homemade chamois-leather loincloth.

'Hold your horses! I've brought a towel to cover you up,' said Gran. 'We've seen enough of you as it is.'

Dad put his loincloth on behind the towel. 'Fire Bird, you have done well.'

'He now looks like **Tarzan**!' said Hero, staring at Dad in his new jungle pants. 'Though at least it covers his backside.'

'Is everything all right?' said a voice. 'Only, I've had reports of someone indulging in extreme fishing on the Rec.'

Hero turned to Mr Harry Bugwell gawping at them from the garden next door. Bugging Bugwell was the last person in the world he wanted to see. He was a short, tubby man with a hooked nose and a small moustache, which he waxed several times a day. A fan of detective stories, he was notorious in Borromeo Road as a self-appointed neighbourhood surveillance officer. Bugwell never missed a trick and received great pleasure in being the messenger of new intelligence – or what other residents called 'gossip'.

'Is that Eddie?' asked Bugwell, leaning over the fence.

'No!' replied Hero, swallowing hard and thinking quickly. 'He's … he's a foreign guest!'

'**Yes!** He's on an exchange and is staying with us for a while,' chipped in Gran.

'That's Eddie Trough; I'd know his skinny body anywhere,' said Bugwell, twiddling one end of his moustache. 'It's very distinctive.'

'Err … we're only pulling your leg,' said Gran with a false laugh.

'He's training for a survival competition,' blurted Hero.

'Very interesting,' said Bugwell. 'He might need to put on some clothes if he wants to survive Heatwave Blistering Bertha. He looks like he's getting burnt.'

'I've got some aloe vera lotion indoors,' said Gran, grabbing Dad's arm and pulling him towards the house. 'It soothes and calms. Quite remarkable really.'

Before Bugwell could ask another question, Hero said, 'Is that your phone? I'm sure I heard it ring.'

'I heard nothing,' said Bugwell with a confused frown.

'You'd better check; it could be important,' said Hero. 'There are fracking protestors coming this way!'

As Bugwell rushed inside, worried he might have missed a call, Hero, Gran and Dad hurried into their own house.

'The whole neighbourhood will know now,' said Hero, plunging himself down on the sofa. 'Oh, Gran. What are we going to do?'

Photos and Places

'This is my baby!' said Mitzy, thrusting a silver tablet into the air. 'And the solution to all your problems!'

It was the next day, and Mitzy and Partha had gathered at Hero's house to help him with his dad problem.

'It has an A9 chip, advanced wireless technology, an integrated operating system and retina display with razor-sharp images,' continued Mitzy.

Hero and Partha exchanged a surprised glance.

Mitzy sat down at the pine table in the dimly lit kitchen, where the blinds had been closed to keep out the sun.

'There are three kinds of memory: immediate, short-term and long-term,' said Mitzy, tapping the tablet as she read out her research. 'Those who suffer head injury have good long-term memories, but can struggle with the other two.'

'He can't remember anything,' said Hero, staring at the screen, which glowed like a mystical oracle.

'Therapists use a variety of techniques to recover memories, such as visual cues, hypnotism, free association, relaxation training and truth serum.'

'Truth serum?' exclaimed Partha. 'Are we in a James Bond movie? Your mission, 007, is to restore the memory of Mr Trough,' he said with a deep voice.

'Shut up, Partha!' said Mitzy.

'What should we try first?' asked Hero impatiently.

'Photographs! They are low-tech memory aids that can help recovery,' said Mitzy, sliding her glasses up her nose.

Hero went into the living room and returned with a thick brown photograph album covered with drawings of Leonardo da Vinci's inventions. He placed it on the wooden table and swept away a thin layer of dust. He then turned back the cover to show a youthful Mum and Dad.

'**Wow!** Have you seen your dad's mullet?' said Partha, looking at the photo with a detached amusement.

Hero stared at the picture of Mum with her sparkling eyes, white smile and porcelain skin. Dad was long-haired and fresh-faced without the tram-track lines on his forehead and flecks of silver that now peppered his hair.

He turned another page.

'Don't tell me that's you!' giggled Partha, pointing to a picture of a naked baby lying on a furry rug.

Beneath the photo was written in faded ink:

Herodotus Carson Cornelius
Da Vinci Einstein Mozart Trough

'**ARRRhhh...** you were so cute!' said Mitzy, leaning over Hero's shoulder to get a closer look. 'But is that your name?'

Hero squirmed.

'It's long.'

'Herodotus?' asked Partha, smirking. 'What kind of name is that?'

'It's Greek!' said Hero. 'He was the father of history.'

'Carson?'

'Some biologist who discovered that pesticides killed birds.'

'Cornelius?' continued Partha with a wide grin.

'After Mr Cuthbert, the guy who wrote the encyclopaedias.'

'Da Vinci?'

'Are we going to do this or not?' snapped Hero, slamming closed the album.

'I want to see more pictures of

H-E-R-O-D-O-T-U-S!'

teased Partha.

'Really, Partha!' said Mitzy, twitching her nose. 'Let's focus on our mission. Now come on!'

Dad sat with his legs crossed on Gran's purple yoga mat in the back garden under the gazebo, out of the gleaming sunlight.

'Do you recognise anyone in these pictures?' asked Hero, showing Dad the album.

'What is this?' said Dad, looking at a page of faded coloured photographs.

'It's a photo,' blurted Mitzy.

'What is ph-o-to?' Dad scowled.

'We'll do a selfie and show you,' said Mitzy, directing Hero and Partha to squeeze in close to Dad.

Mitzy held her tablet in front of them; an image of their faces appeared on the screen.

Dad examined the picture through narrowed eyes, then jumped back in fear.

'You have spirits of our ancestors in there,' he said.

Mitzy and Partha giggled at Dad's reaction.

'It's not a spirit,' said Hero, not wanting to upset Dad. First with the car and now the tablet. It seemed Dad didn't understand technology.

'Have you seen these?' He pointed to other photographs in the album to distract Dad. 'Do you recognise anyone?'

Dad studied the photos, including one of himself dressed in a brown checked suit and flared trousers at cousin Eloisa's wedding. 'I know none of these people,' he said.

'Are you sure?' asked Mitzy, frowning.

'What about this woman?' said Hero, pointing to a picture of Mum.

Dad hesitated and moved his face closer to the picture. Hero hoped Dad would recognise Mum and remember.

'She is fine-looking, but I do not know her,' he said.

Partha turned the page of the album.

'What about this baby?' he asked.

'I do not know this child,' replied Dad.

Hero gave a disappointed **huff**. It was clear

Dad remembered no one, not even himself.

'What are his favourite places?' said Mitzy, undeterred by the setback.

Hero bit the side of his lip and stared up at the cloudless blue sky for inspiration.

'I guess … it's got to be … his study, allotment and … the central library.'

'Well, he's already been in the study, so that probably won't work, and the library closed down last month, so the only thing left is his allotment,' said Mitzy.

'Come on!'

'Wait … but … err … we should pretend he's training for a survival competition or something,' Hero said, running after her. 'Otherwise people will think he's really weird.'

Red Earth

A little while later, they all arrived at Oak Lane allotments, where Hero used to go with his parents on Sunday afternoons. Mum was so proud of her home-grown produce she entered them in the Leaford Show. One year she won a silver certificate for her broad beans and was determined to win gold – but then she fell ill.

Dad leaned on his brush-handle spear and surveyed a hard, dry patch of soil scattered with yellow, wilting plants.

'I do not know this place,' he said.

'Are you sure?' said Hero. He held his breath, hoping something would jog Dad's memory.

'This land is new to me,' said Dad with a pensive gaze. He bent down and pulled up a clump of dried leaves; soil beneath the roots crumbled into dust. 'This earth needs to be fed. It is turning red.'

'I do hope we get some rain soon; otherwise, my babies will shrivel up and die,' said a voice.

They all turned to see Miss Petula Flowerdew, Leaford's green-fingered celebrity famed for her marrows, which were the largest and tastiest in the region.

'Is that you, Eddie?' she asked.

Miss Flowerdew leaned over the broken wooden fence and squinted through her golden-rimmed, yellow-tinted glasses on the tip of her nose. 'I haven't seen you in ages.'

'He's been training for a survival competition,' said Hero with a nervous smile.

'I can see he's changed,' she said, her eyes fixed on Dad's chamois-leather loincloth.

Partha peeked over the fence at the large green torpedo-shaped vegetables basking under a net canopy. 'Your marrows look fine to me.'

'That's because I've been nourishing my babies with my yellow milk.'

'What's that?' said Partha, frowning.

Miss Flowerdew gave a mischievous grin. 'Don't you know what yellow milk is?' she said.

'You don't mean …' said Mitzy, her eyes widening.

'I do … but keep it quiet.'

'What is it?' asked Partha, confused.

'It's pee!' declared Hero. 'Dad told me pee is full of nutrients and acts like a fertiliser.'

Partha screwed up his face in disgust. 'That's gross!'

'We should go back,' said Hero. 'It's too hot.' It was clear they were getting nowhere fast.

'**Wait!** Little Shadow,' said Dad, raising his hand in the air, 'we must first help this elder.'

'How?'

'This elder needs to nourish her body and feed her children. We must create rain for her.'

'Create rain?' exclaimed Hero. The heat was definitely making Dad's behaviour worse.

'What did he say?' said Miss Flowerdew, cupping her ear with her hand.

'Nothing, he's just mumbling.'

'The mighty sun is strong,' said Dad, signalling to the sky. 'We need to get the clouds to work for us.'

'I bet he wants to do a rain dance,' gasped Partha.

'**Err ... NO ... WAY,**' said Hero, baffled at the suggestion.

'A rain dance?' said Miss Flowerdew. 'I guess we've got nothing to lose, especially if it helps me win the Leaford Show.'

'Elder, do not fear,' said Dad confidently. 'The rain

will come, you will have food to nourish your weary body and feed your offspring.'

Miss Flowerdew gave a broad smile, drawing back her cheeks like curtains, making her wrinkles disappear.

'We must call on the clouds to create the rain.'

'It's pointless. My weather app shows we're going to have a heatwave for weeks,' said Mitzy adamantly.

Hero was now regretting coming to the allotment. It was bad enough Dad walking around half naked in a chamois-leather loincloth, never mind him dancing and trying to make it rain. The words of Dr Anagnostopoulos came flying back into his head like an unwelcome boomerang.

'Come! I must walk,' said Dad, marching off along the path.

Hero frowned at Mitzy. 'The doctor said we've got to let him recover naturally. I guess we have no choice,' he said, chasing after Dad.

'This will be interesting,' said Mitzy.

Miss Flowerdew climbed onto her metallic-pink mobility scooter covered in faded coloured rosettes. Bundles of green beans wrapped up in old copies of the *Leaford Bugle* overflowed from the front basket.

'**Wait for me!** I'm not going to miss this for all the leeks in Leaford,' she said.

Rain Chant

Hero and the others followed Dad as he marched along with his head down in deep thought and his homemade spear in his hand. It wasn't long before they arrived at number 32 Borromeo Road, where they entered the back garden.

Hero hurried into the house. If he had to do some kind of rain dance, then he was going to make sure he did it properly. And where better to learn out how to do a rain dance than in Cuthbert's encyclopaedia.

Hero went into Dad's study and read entry number 23844: 'CEREMONIAL DANCES'. Armed with this new information, he returned to the back garden to find Dad alone with Miss Flowerdew.

'Where are the others?' he asked, eager to get the whole thing over with.

'They've gone for a few important supplies,' said Miss Flowerdew, her eyes twinkling with excitement. 'They shouldn't be long.'

'Little Shadow, we need something for our foreheads to soak up the body's moisture,' said Dad thoughtfully. 'We must concentrate hard if we are to get the clouds to work for us.'

Hero had an idea. He ran into the house and returned a few minutes later with a tie-dyed scarf and three coloured, thin leather ties that Dad had at the back of the wardrobe from his student days.

Dad checked out Hero's offering and smiled. 'You have done well, Little Shadow.'

Dad took the scarf that had all the colours of the rainbow. He tied it round his brow, letting the ends hang loose at the side of his face. He then put an electric-blue tie round Hero's head.

Hero forced a smile. If it were as simple as doing a dance to make it rain, the weatherman would do a jig every time there was a drought. But Hero had to go along with it, especially if it helped Dad to get better.

He scanned the perimeter of the fence, hoping Mr Bugwell wasn't watching.

'Exactly as you requested, Mr Trough … err …

sorry … Terra Firma,' said Mitzy, entering the garden with Partha.

Mitzy smiled proudly and handed Dad a set of amethyst gemstone beads.

'They used to be my granny's. They're selling similar necklaces online for fifty pounds. So don't lose them.'

Dad placed the gemstones around his neck.

'I've got this,' said Partha, eager to see Dad's response. He held a large white ostrich feather. 'It was the only feather in the house. My dad bought it for a fancy dress at New Year from Spirit and Spice, that New Age stall on Leaford market.'

Dad studied the feather and smiled broadly. He then placed it in the side of his headscarf.

Hero sucked in a breath, for Dad now looked really strange. Was this what an earth warrior was supposed to wear?

- **MUSTARD CHAMOIS-LEATHER LOINCLOTH**
- **RAINBOW HEADSCARF WITH A WHITE OSTRICH FEATHER**
- **AMETHYST BEADS**
- **WOODEN BROOM-HANDLE SPEAR WITH A KITCHEN KNIFE TIED TO THE END WITH GREEN GARDENING STRING**
- **UNION FLAG FLIP-FLOPS**

Dad squared his shoulders and drew himself up to full height. 'You have all done well,' he said. 'Now let us begin.'

Miss Flowerdew got comfy in a striped deckchair under the gazebo. Hero and Partha grudgingly removed their T-shirts so they could feel Mother Earth's energy. Partha put a lime-green leather tie around his forehead and Mitzy a bright yellow one.

'This will capture the wind,' said Dad, pointing to the ostrich feather on his head. 'And these stones will bring out our inner strength so we can heal this dry earth and help our elder.'

'What are you doing?' Hero said as Dad took hold of his hand.

'We first must create a circle.'

Hero frowned. 'Why?' This was nothing like the entry he had read in Cuthbert's encyclopaedia.

'The circle will combine our energies and connect us to the **web of life**.'

Mitzy gave a puzzled look. 'I've heard of the worldwide web, a spider's web and even Charlotte's web, but never the web of life.'

'All things are connected on this planet,' said Dad, raising his hands in the air. 'Mother Earth has given a role to everything. Joined together, we are strong. But if we are not careful, we could destroy the precious, delicate strands in the web of life. If there are many holes, then the web will become ruined forever, and we will no longer be able to exist.'

'That's really heavy, Mr T.,' said Partha. '**Oops** … sorry … Terra Firma.'

'Come, give me your hand,' said Dad, grabbing Partha.

They all stood holding hands in a circle.

'It won't work!' scoffed Mitzy.

'If the rain doesn't come, it means you have not tapped into your inner energy,' said Dad in a serious tone. 'There is no limit to what we can do when we combine our energies in the web of life.'

Hero just wanted Dad to hurry up before Bugwell found out what they were doing.

Dad closed his eyes and hummed in a soft tone, his face calm in meditation.

Hero glanced at Partha, who had tightened his lips, trying hard not to burst out laughing. Hero ignored him, put his head down and purred quietly.

After a while, a blissful sensation swept over Hero like the joy of a thousand Christmases. As the feeling became stronger, his doubts, worries and fears melted away.

They all *swayed* from *side* to *side*. Then Dad said,

'LET THE WHITE floating clouds
DELIVER THE RAIN SO THE ELDERS OF
THE EARTH CAN EAT AGAIN.

LIGHTNING!

THUNDER!

RAINBOW TOO!

LET THE clouds WORK FOR ME AND YOU.'

Hero and the others learned the words and became immersed in the hypnotic chants and rhythmic movements. Meanwhile, Miss Flowerdew snored away in the deckchair with her mouth wide open.

After about twenty minutes, someone yelled, 'WHAT THE DICKENS ARE YOU DOING?'

Hero caught sight of Gran standing on the kitchen doorstep with her hands on her hips.

'What a spectacle!' said a deep voice. Mr Bugwell appeared at the fence.

As soon as Gran clocked her nosy neighbour, she ran down the garden waving her hands in the air.

'That's enough! It's too hot to continue!'

Hero collapsed on the dried-up lawn, ruby-faced and breathless, his eyes swirling.

'**Wow!**' gasped Partha. 'That was super incredible!'

'I don't believe it,' said Mitzy, baffled. 'My whole body was not mine. I kept going round and round.'

Dad stood still with his head bowed, mumbling to himself.

'I was a bird flying high in the sky,' Hero said with a smile stretched across his sweaty face.

'What are you all doing dressed like that out here in this heat?' said Gran, shattering their moment of joy.

'We've done a rain chant!' said Hero proudly.

'It was wicked,' chimed in Partha.

'Very nice, but we should all go in now,' said Gran with a furrowed brow.

Miss Flowerdew grunted before opening her eyes. 'Have you finished already?' She took off her straw hat, then wiped her wizened forehead with a dirty grey handkerchief.

'When does the rain come?' she asked, curious.

'We must wait, and we shall see if the clouds respond to our call,' said Dad.

'Let's go in and have some lemonade,' said Gran, signalling them to the kitchen.

As they passed the fence, Mr Bugwell looked up and down at what they were wearing.

'Isn't your father too old to be playing ring-a-ring o' roses in fancy dress?' he said.

Before Hero could reply, Partha said, 'We've just done a rain chant. So don't put your washing out, mister!'

'Rain? We could do with some of that. If you can make it rain, you'll be on the front cover of the *Leaford Bugle* next to the flying pigs!' chuckled Mr Bugwell.

Cumulonimbus

'Your father will be a laughing stock now him next door has seen the shenanigans of today,' said Gran. She stood in the kitchen with her arms crossed and lips pursed tight.

'I did what the doctor told us,' said Hero, his voice raising an octave. 'I went along with his world.'

After all, it wasn't his fault Dad took pity on old Miss Flowerdew's marrows and decided to do a rain chant.

'Oh … I wish I had some Zumbi brew,' huffed Gran.

'What's that?' said Hero, baffled by the unusual name.

'When I was in Mozambique, I met a Zulu witch doctor with a wonky eye,' said Gran. 'He claimed his concoction could cure anything. I didn't taste it, though. I heard he was looking for another wife. He seemed to have taken quite a fancy to me. But that bulbous eye! Gives me goosebumps just thinking about it watching me. He wanted—'

'I'd … better get back to the others,' said Hero, escaping from Gran's tales to the living room.

There, Mitzy, Partha, Miss Flowerdew and Dad stood at the bay window, gazing up at the darkening sky.

'Look at that grey cloud,' pointed Partha.

'It's getting **bigger**!' observed Mitzy.

Miss Flowerdew took off her glasses and squinted hard. 'Why, you're right. That's the funniest-looking cloud I've ever seen.'

Hero rushed across the room to join them and looked up at the dark formations.

'That's a **cumulonimbus**!' he said, raising his eyebrows.

'How do you know?' Mitzy asked.

'My dad told me,' boasted Hero. 'When you see that, then a big storm is coming.'

'I've got a weather app,' said Mitzy, raising her nose. 'I'll check later.'

Hero smiled, content that one of Dad's boring facts had impressed his friends, even if Mitzy didn't quite believe him.

Dad nodded contentedly. 'The clouds are working for our elders.'

Gran came marching into the living room. 'What are you all doing?'

'It's going to rain!' marvelled Hero.

Gran bent towards the window and peered up at the sky. 'Well, knock me over with an ostrich feather. You've done it!'

The cloud puffed outwards until it looked like an enormous smoky-grey meringue. This was followed by an

'Come on!' said Hero excitedly. 'Let's see if it's going to rain.'

They all followed him into the back garden where the rumbling got louder and louder until it sounded as if a million pan lids were being smashed together.

CRACK!

A bolt of lightning shot across the darkened sky. 'Wow!' gasped Partha.

Hero gaped at the sight of the spectacle. There was a volcanic boom, then hard rain came pouring down.

'Yippppeeeeee!

We've done it!' said Hero, jumping for joy.

They all cheered as cool, refreshing droplets bathed their faces and bodies. The rain hit the parched ground, transforming the garden into a sea of puddles.

Next door, Mr Bugwell stopped tending his lawn when the first raindrops fell on the tip of his protruding nose. 'I don't believe it!' he said, hurrying inside to make a phone call.

Miss Flowerdew took off her hat and used her grey handkerchief like a flannel to wash her face.

'It's a miracle!' she squeaked, turning to Dad. 'It may even save my babies. You must help us with our protest on the Rec. We need supporters with your talent. Let's have a chat later.'

Hero grinned so much his cheeks ached. Dad, who wasn't good at anything practical, had done the impossible. He had made it RAIN!

Breaking News

'Hero! Hero! Get up!'

It was the next morning, and Gran was yelling up the stairs. Half asleep, Hero opened his eyes just enough to see his football alarm clock flashing 7.35. He gave a humungous yawn, scratched his head and hauled himself out of bed.

Raindrops **rapped** against the window. The downpour had continued all night and showed no sign of relenting. Hero stumbled across the room and flung back the curtains to find a large white van with a satellite dish on the top parked slap-bang in front of his house.

'Nooooooooo Waaaaaaay!'

The vehicle had Globe News emblazoned in bold blue letters along its side. A reporter stood in the rain, holding a big umbrella and talking to a camera.

'Hero!' yelled Gran again.

Hero hurried downstairs to find Gran in the hall, looking much older than usual. 'Globe News want to speak with your father.'

Hero swallowed hard.

'The *Bugle* tipped them off,' said Gran, letting out a breath. 'I told them it was a load of baloney. No one would ever believe our Eddie caused the rain. But they were so insistent I had to agree to the interview. It's a good human-interest story. Just what they're looking for: to spice up the dull news agenda. We're on after the eight o'clock headlines.'

Hero stood dazed in the hall. He may have wanted Dad to stop being a boring bookworm, but appearing live on national TV was something else.

'I need to go. All this excitement is not good for my bladder,' said Gran, hurrying to the stairs. 'Your father is in the kitchen – make sure he stays there.'

KNOCK, KNOCK, KNOCK!

A dark shadow with a hat appeared at the front door. Hero peered through the letterbox.

'I'm getting soaked,' said Mr Bugwell. 'Are you going to let me in?'

Hero opened the door.

'Can you believe it?' said Bugwell, entering the hall. 'Robin Rivett, the award-winning roving reporter, is in Borromeo Road.' Droplets of rain dripped down his face and slid along his aquiline nose.

Hero smiled nervously.

'I've a copy of the *Bugle* for your gran. I bought ten copies, so don't worry, you won't have to give it back.'

Hero squirmed at the sight of the headline:

LEAFORD'S EARTH WARRIOR CAUSES RAIN

'He's made the front page!' exclaimed Mr Bugwell, pointing at a photograph of Dad in his warrior outfit.

Hero wasn't sure how they got the photo but suspected it had something to do with Bugwell's surveillance cameras. Either way, it didn't feel right.

Beside the picture was another breaking-news headline:

FIGHTBACK BEGINS ON FRACKING FIELD

'Protestors have set up an illegal camp on the Rec,' said Bugwell, twitching with excitement. 'It's all happening in Leaford. On page two there's a photo of yours truly.'

Hero turned the page and cringed at the image of Mr Bugwell leaning on the front gate with the headline:

EYEWITNESS ACCOUNT OF LEAFORD'S EARTH WARRIOR RAIN CHANT

'I impressed the journalist with my levels of observation and eye for detail,' said Mr Bugwell proudly. 'Although the photographer hasn't done me justice. I look like a chipmunk!'

Before Hero could respond, Mr Bugwell was halfway back out of the front door.

'I've got to dash. They're going to interview me on Globe News. I need to prepare my moustache. Cheerio,' he said.

As soon as Mr Bugwell left, Gran appeared. 'What did that busybody want?'

Hero looked down at the paper in his hand. Gran clocked the headline.

'No wonder it's a good story,' said Gran, arching her pencil-thin eyebrows. 'We'd better inform your father. You know how the media likes to sensationalise things. We can't have any more of this **silliness**.'

Hero followed Gran into the kitchen where Dad was sitting on the yoga mat with his legs crossed and his eyes closed in mournful meditation, surrounded by a circle of coloured gemstones.

'We need to talk,' said Gran with urgency in her voice. 'The TV people want to interview you about the rain chant.'

Dad opened his eyes slowly. 'The clouds are working hard for us. The youth tapped into the web of life.'

'Don't say too much,' implored Hero. After the

rain chant, Hero was tingling with excitement, but the thought of everyone knowing what they had done made his stomach churn as if it had just been put on a fast spin.

'I will be truthful at all times and under all conditions,' said Dad. He closed his eyes and smiled.

KNOCK, KNOCK, KNOCK!

'They're here!' yelled Hero.

'Go and get dressed,' gasped Gran. 'We can't have the whole nation seeing you in your jim-jams!'

Media Sensation

A little while later, Hero **stomped** downstairs to find the living room a hive of media activity. The last time he had seen the house so busy was when Mum had a coffee morning to raise funds for the local hospice.

'Right, Mrs Trough, you sit on the sofa here with your son next to you,' said a rotund man with a high-pitched voice. 'Robin will be seated in that chair there.'

He held a clipboard in one hand and a pen in the other, which he used as an extended finger to prod people.

'Who is that?' he said, pointing at Hero.

'That's my grandson,' squeaked Gran.

'I'm Baggins, the producer. Can you sit here?' he said, signalling to the arm of the sofa.

Hero followed the instruction.

'Brett, will they all be in the frame if we put the boy on the end?'

A tall blond man behind a camera on a tripod stuck his thumb up.

Baggins tapped his pen on his clipboard.

'Right, listen up. Take your places, everyone,' he shouted, trying to appear masterly. 'Please bring in the famous earth warrior.'

Dad entered the living room wearing his chamois-leather loincloth, rainbow-coloured headscarf, white ostrich feather, amethyst-bead necklace and holding his homemade broom-handle spear.

Everyone stopped what they were doing and stared, and for a few seconds all that could be heard was the rain tapping against the window.

Hero felt his cheeks grow hot.

'Mrs Trough, your son is a fine figure of a warrior!' screeched Baggins.

'Can you sit here, Mr Trough?' he said, pointing his pen to the sofa.

'I am Terra Firma,' said Dad in a strong, proud voice. 'An earth warrior.'

'Robin, can you have a chat with the family about what you want to ask them?' said Baggins, intimidated by Dad's presence.

Robin Rivett adjusted his eyepatch and patted his ink-black beard before going over to Hero, Dad and Gran on the sofa.

'Sorry for all this early-morning intrusion,' he said.

Hero grinned nervously at seeing the award-winning roving reporter Robin Rivett up close and in person. He looked shorter and slimmer than on the TV.

'It's wonderful to see you, Robin ... sorry, Mr Rivett,' said Gran, blushing under her suntan. 'I woke up with you every day for years when you were on breakfast TV. It's as if you're a member of the family.'

Robin gave a dazzling white smile that eclipsed his black whiskers. 'I'm pleased to meet you. Now, I will ask three simple questions: why, when and how you created the rain,' he said.

'Take your places,' bellowed Baggins from across the room. 'We're going live in ten seconds.'

'SILENCE!'

Baggins counted down. Rivett fiddled with his earpiece before talking to the camera.

'Alistair, I'm here once again in Leaford, which only a few days ago experienced the highest temperatures in the country due to Heatwave Blistering Bertha. But the city is now encountering torrential rain and thunderstorms, which have been allegedly caused by Leaford's very own earth warrior.'

Rivett turned to Dad. 'Terra Firma, is it true you made it rain?'

Dad closed his eyes and hummed. **'Ammmmmmmmmmmmmmm.'**

'Are you all right?' said Rivett, astounded by the response.

'I'm tuning in to the web of life,' said Dad.

'Well, our viewers are tuning in now to see how you created the rain.'

Dad stopped humming, opened his eyes and smiled proudly. 'We used our inner energy to send a message to the clouds.'

Hero grinned at the camera as blood rushed to his cheeks and a warm flutter tickled his insides. For the first time in ages, he felt **special**.

'It was fantastic!' he blurted.

'Really?' asked Robin with an incredulous smirk. 'How did you make it rain?'

'We chanted in a circle,' said Hero, gushing with enthusiasm.

'Thank you, but please let Terra Firma answer.'

'The boy is right. We did a rain chant and tapped into the web of life—'

'It was amazing,' interrupted Hero.

'Well the clouds certainly have been working for you,' said Rivett with a false smile.

He turned to Gran. 'Mrs Trough, I'm sure you're very proud of your warrior son with such unusual powers?'

'We're very proud,' added Hero.

'How have you coped all these years, thinking you'd lost him?'

'Lost him? He's never been anywhere!' said Gran, tightening the lines on her face, glancing at Rivett and then at the camera.

Rivett squished his black eyebrows together like kissing caterpillars. 'Are you saying you didn't lose your son on a motorbiking trip when he was a baby, only for him to turn up years later as an earth warrior?'

'You've been watching too many soaps!' exclaimed Gran, shaking her head. 'Our Eddie is a Leaford lad, born and bred. He's never been abroad, not since we took him to the Isle of Man. That's when he suffered from seasickness. I think it scarred him for life. Although I blame it on those whelks he ate. I told his father he was too young, but—'

'Mrs Trough, are you saying the earth warrior is not a real warrior?'

'Of course not,' frowned Gran. 'He's only been doing this warrior malarkey for about a week now.'

Hero scowled. His stomach suddenly felt ice cold. This wasn't good at all.

Rivett pressed his earpiece again. Baggins pointed his pen at him, indicating he was to continue. He turned to Dad with glee, knowing he was onto a breaking-news story.

'How can you claim to be an earth warrior?' growled Rivett. 'Is this all a joke?'

Hero's heart pounded in his head at the prospect of Dad being revealed as a charlatan, a fake and a hoaxer – nothing more than his **boring dad**.

'Being an earth warrior isn't blood,' said Dad in an earnest tone. 'It is the life we all carry deep inside ourselves.'

He stared at the camera. 'It is the truth in our heart and connection with nature.'

He placed his hand on his chest. 'It is about honour, love and respect.'

In a strong, slow authoritarian voice, he said, 'Honour, love and respect Mother Earth; honour, love and respect the web of life; honour, love and respect each other and all things – **THAT** is what it is to be an earth warrior.'

Rivett was lost for words, taken aback by Dad's conviction. 'Err … what are your plans, now you have created rain?' he asked, wanting to move on to cover his silence.

'Heaven is our father, Earth is our mother and all things are our brothers and sisters,' said Dad.

Hero glared at Dad, confused. He'd never heard Dad talk like this.

'I will set up camp and gather my tribe of earth warriors,' continued Dad. 'Together we will fight to protect Mother Earth, who is in danger from the grey man.'

At that point, Baggins stuck out his pen and made circular movements.

'Sorry, we're running out of time. Thank you for speaking with us today. That's all from Leaford. Now back to Alistair in the studio.'

'Thanks, everybody,' yelled Baggins, piercing the air with his screechy voice. 'Let's get out of here. We have an interview next door. Then we need to pop in and see what the fracking protestors are up to if no other story breaks.'

Baggins skipped across the room towards Hero and Dad.

Wonderful!
Absolutely wonderful!

What a mesmerising performance. You have real presence and charisma,' he said. 'After today you'll be a media sensation. People will be flocking to see you. Mark my words, Baggins is never wrong!'

Visitors

'I don't know when all this bother is going to end,' said Gran later that morning. 'It's been more than a week now, and your father doesn't look like he's getting any better.'

She marched off into the kitchen, her head bobbing from side to side.

Hero's chest tightened at the thought that Dad would never recover. What if he would always walk around half naked in a chamois-leather loincloth? That would be a million times worse than Dad reading his books every passing hour.

Hero went over to the living-room window. The Globe News people had gone and Borromeo Road was awash with rainwater. He let out a deep breath before taking the remote control, collapsing in the armchair and zapping on the TV.

Dramatic music boomed from the speaker as

BREAKING NEWS

flashed across the screen.

'The Environment Agency has issued a severe flood warning for Leaford due to the torrential rain. The River Leaf has broken its banks, flooding over six hundred homes. Up to a thousand people have been forced to take refuge in local schools, church halls and sports centres. Now over to our award-winning roving reporter, Robin Rivett,' said Alistair Homes.

Gran marched back into the living room and stared at the TV screen, her arms wrapped around her body.

Rivett was standing outside the white-brick Victorian town hall wearing a raincoat and wellington boots and holding a blue Globe News umbrella.

'Alistair, the situation in Leaford has taken a turn for the worse, with severe flooding now affecting large parts of the city. Let's hear how they're coping from Chief Councillor Erik Onions.'

The drenched face of the council leader, with his multiple chins, filled the screen.

Hero scowled at the TV.

'What are you doing to address the flooding?' asked Rivett.

'Well, we've been providing sand bags to high-risk neighbourhoods and food and shelter to those who had to evacuate their homes,' said Chief Councillor Onions with a proud smile that made him look like an overblown balloon.

'We're also advising everyone to keep their bathing costumes on, just in case they have to swim to safety.'

'Are you aware one of your employees is masquerading as an earth warrior and claiming to have caused this extraordinary downpour?' said Rivett.

'Absolute nonsense!' replied Onions, wiping droplets of rain from his thinning hair. 'It's not true. I'm afraid he's another victim of this horrendous heat – we're all suffering at the council, you know.'

'So, you're saying it's acceptable for your workers to go doolally?'

'No, I never said that!' protested the councillor. 'I merely—'

'Sorry, we're running out of time.'

'Yes, but I—'

'Thank you, Chief Councillor Onions,' said Rivett with a menacing smile. 'Now back to Alistair in the studio.'

KNOCK, KNOCK, KNOCK!

Hero entered the hall and peered through the opaque glass of the front door at two dark silhouettes. He gave a dramatic sigh of relief when he opened it to find Mitzy and Partha standing there.

'We've seen you all on TV,' said Mitzy, huddled under an umbrella.

'It's turning into a big mess,' said Hero, leading them to the study.

'Why? Your dad's going to be famous,' said Partha. 'People will ask him for his autograph. He might even get his own TV show one day.'

For a moment, Hero stared into space, computing what he had just seen on the TV. 'The rain has caused flooding. It's all over the news,' he said pensively.

'Everyone has been wanting it to rain for weeks,' replied Partha.

'Don't you see we're responsible for all those people losing their homes?'

'It ain't our fault the rain came all at once,' said Partha, raising his voice.

Hero clenched his jaw. It was easy for Partha to dismiss his part in the rain chant.

'I have found something else we can try,' said Mitzy, holding up her tablet. 'We could—'

'What is it?' said Hero eagerly.

'A truth serum!'

'A truth serum?' Hero tilted his head. 'Do such things exist?'

'Yes! I've found a recipe to make one on the internet.'

'But Dad isn't lying. How can a truth serum help him get his memory back?'

'Truth serum helps people recover their memory,' said Mitzy, sitting on the edge of the armchair. 'All our memories are held in the brain's filing system. A hit to the head can lock the filing system. The truth serum will unlock the cabinets of the mind so your dad can remember who he is.'

'What's in this truth serum?' asked Hero, intrigued.

'We need a South African plant called kanna,' said Mitzy.

'Are you mad?' sneered Hero. 'There's no way we can get the money to go to South Africa.'

'I'll ask Miss Flowerdew to help,' said Mitzy, raising her chin in the air. 'She grows all sorts of things.'

'Yes, marrows, carrots, potatoes and courgettes – not some exotic plant from Africa!' said Hero.

'There's always the botanical gardens,' chimed in Partha. 'They have a whole dome devoted to Africa. We've been there with Scouts. It was really cool – or should I say hot?'

'We can't steal it,' said Mitzy with a disapproving frown. 'That wouldn't be right.'

'It depends how much you need,' said Partha. 'Nobody will notice if a few leaves go missing.'

'It's still wrong.'

'It won't work,' said Hero, remembering what his teacher Mr Roxburgh had said about not believing everything you read on the internet.

Mitzy scowled. 'I'll ask Miss Flowerdew anyway. She knows someone who works at the botanical gardens.'

'Do what you want,' snapped Hero.

'Good! We all agree then,' said Mitzy with a triumphant smile. 'We'll try the truth serum!'

'Who's that now?' huffed Hero. He opened the front door just enough to see.

'Is Mrs Trough at home?' said a deep voice.

Before Hero had time to reply, Gran appeared. 'I'm Mrs Trough senior. How can I help you?'

'I'm Chief Inspector Craddock and this is Mr Slapnatch from Leaford social services. I wonder if we could have a word with you and Mr Trough.'

Slapnatch

Hero sat on the sofa leaning forward, keen to hear what the chief inspector had to say.

'You are a chief?' asked Dad from the armchair.

'I am indeed,' replied Chief Inspector Craddock. He was a ginger-haired man with a barrel of a belly straining to be released from his blue short-sleeved shirt.

'What is the name of your tribe?'

'Tribe?' said Inspector Craddock, confused. 'I'm from the police.'

'One day I will have my own tribe in this land,' said Dad with a dreamy gaze.

'Let's get down to business, shall we? Chief Councillor Onions has asked me to pay you a visit,' said the chief inspector. He coughed into his hand.

'It's an unusual request, but being chief councillor

and all, and a close friend of my boss, the police commissioner – let's say … we couldn't refuse.'

'What are you talking about?' said Gran, squeezing her hands together.

'It's about Mr Trough claiming to cause the torrential rain we've had here in Leaford.'

'It's not his fault!' blurted Hero, not wanting to be in trouble with the police. After all, they never expected the chant to work. The rain could be down to a freak weather event – a result of global warming, for example.

'It's unlikely that you caused the rain,' said the chief inspector. 'But when people get something in their head, that's how rumours start.'

'What is your concern, chief?' asked Dad, looking the inspector in the eye.

'The chief councillor is anxious that all this media attention is bad for the reputation of the city. He's unhappy that a council employee is going around claiming to have caused the flooding. Over six hundred people needed to abandon their homes, you know. Now, if they think the council was responsible … well … that wouldn't be good, would it? The local elections are not far off.'

Hero squeezed his lips together, holding in the

words. The sooner Onions was voted out of the office, the better.

'It is sad when you lose your home,' said Dad, raising a brow of concern. 'If we do not take care of Mother Earth, we could all lose our home.'

'You'll understand then; it would be good for the city, and your future employment, if you stopped claiming to have created the rain. In particular, no more media interviews,' said Inspector Craddock.

'You haven't one shred of evidence that my son caused the rain,' said Gran, rising from the sofa in protest.

'He's had a bang to the head,' piped up Hero. 'He's sick; you can ask Dr Anagnostopoulos at Leaford General.'

'And that's another thing we're concerned about,' said the inspector. 'I'll let Mr Slapnatch explain.'

Mr Slapnatch grinned like a weasel, with his two yellowish front teeth protruding from his lips.

'Due to Mr Trough's illness, we think it is advisable to have a planned break at this time of particular stress,' he said.

Hero frowned hard, unsure what the rodent man was talking about.

'You mean take Dad away?' asked Hero weakly.

'He'll recover better at home,' said Gran. 'You can pick up all sorts of bugs in hospital. When I went in for an operation for my haemorrhoids—'

'I'm talking about Herodotus Trough,' snapped Slapnatch.

'Take me away?' said Hero, stunned at the thought.

'It will only be a short while, until your father recovers. There's a nice foster family who'll take care of you. If that doesn't work out, we can always find a place at Miss Callous's Residential Care Home for Wayward Kids.'

Slapnatch grinned and nibbled his lips.

'His dad may be away with the fairies, but I'm still here,' said Gran, her nostrils flaring.

Mr Slapnatch made a sound that was somewhere between a laugh and a cough. Whatever it was, his breath stank.

'Social services have a statutory obligation to safeguard and promote the welfare of vulnerable children. Chief Councillor Onions is concerned about this case,' said Slapnatch, wringing his greasy paws. 'It is admirable that you want to take care of your grandson, but it's too much for you at your age.'

'I am not vulnerable and don't need protecting!' said Hero, the suggestion stinging like a bee.

Gran made one of her 'you ain't gonna mess with me' faces.

'Listen here,
hamster features!'

she said. 'I may be a vintage model, but there's still life in this old gal. You're not taking my grandson anywhere, whether it's your statutory duty or not!'

Slapnatch recoiled back into the chair. 'If we get a court order, you'll have no choice!' he growled, his face turning reddish orange.

'Can we all calm down?' said the chief inspector, splaying his freckled hands in the air. 'If Mr Trough recovers, then this will not be necessary. The sooner the rain stops, the better for everyone.'

At that moment, Dad, who had been sitting in silence and observing, said solemnly, 'I understand, chief. I honour and respect your word and will do what I need to do.'

'I'm pleased you're willing to cooperate,' said Craddock, nodding with a grin. 'Well, that's all for now.'

'In the meantime, I'll make the necessary preparations,' snarled Slapnatch. 'I think the boy would benefit from a stay at Miss Callous's care home.'

A Wonderful Assignment

'We've got to stop this rain as soon as possible,' said Hero urgently. He wasn't sure whether another chant would work, but they had to try something; otherwise, Craddock and Slapnatch would be back.

Dad stood up and straightened his shoulders. 'Gather the youth once again. We must ask the clouds to rest now.'

Hero barged into the kitchen, where Mitzy and Partha had been waiting. 'We need to end the rain before the flooding gets any worse and before they take me into care.'

'If we fail, will we go into care too?' said Partha, wiping biscuit crumbs from his face.

'Really!' scowled Mitzy. 'They can't do that. How were we to know it would work?'

'You don't have a dad who has upset Onions and thinks he's a warrior!' said Hero, irritated by Mitzy's remark.

'What about the truth serum?' Partha enquired. 'We need to find Miss Flowerdew and ask her for help to get your dad back to normal.'

At that moment, Dad and Gran appeared. 'Come, youth, we must call on the clouds again to stop their work,' Dad said.

'You did it once; you can do it again,' said Gran with an encouraging smile.

Hero, Mitzy and Partha exchanged a look of trepidation.

The garden spotlight illuminated the dark sky, turning raindrops into falling golden daggers. Hero, Mitzy and Partha stood under the gazebo wearing their headbands, but this time water sloshed around their ankles.

They all formed a circle holding hands. Dad then hummed. Hero felt a tingling feeling in one hand shoot up his arm, across his back and down the other arm and hand. The sensation grew stronger as they *swayed* from *side* to *side*.

Dad recited the words of the incantation backwards.

'LET THE clouds WORK FOR ME AND YOU.

RAINBOW TOO!

ThUNDeR!

LIGHTNING!

LET THE WHITE floating clouds
DELIVER THE RAIN SO THE ELDERS OF
THE EARTH CAN EAT AGAIN.'

Hero opened his mouth, convinced he would fail.
But his body was electrified, and he said all the words
in the correct order.

In the garden next door, there was a movement in
the bushes. Mr Bugwell was hiding, hunched beside
the fence in an army camouflage jacket and a large

green waterproof hat covered in leaves. He held a small video camera given to him by Globe News, who promised another interview if he got exclusive footage.

'I sensed that you tapped into your core energy,' said Dad after they had stopped chanting.

Hero felt as drained as an overused battery. He looked at the pale faces of Mitzy and Partha, who seemed equally wiped out.

Dad gave a satisfied grin. 'The clouds will rest now.' He bowed his head and mumbled a few words. As he did so, Mr Bugwell hurried into his house.

That night Hero went to bed exhausted, hoping the chant would work – as he never wanted to see hamster features again.

The next morning, Hero was relieved to find the rain had stopped just as Dad had predicted. Gran took the opportunity to go out for a ride with the Harley Gals to the Helmet and Wheel for tea and cake.

Hero gazed up at the cloudless sky from the living-room window, wondering whether he had been involved in some kind of meteorological magic. The sun beamed brightly, its rays hitting the ground, causing the water to evaporate and disappear. The grass was now green and lush once again.

He zapped on the TV as he crunched his cornflakes, sitting in the armchair. Globe News's presenter Alistair Homes declared, 'Viewers may remember the unbelievable story of the Leaford council worker turned earth warrior who claimed to have done a rain chant and caused the worst downpour in a decade. Well, he's had a change of heart and has now stopped the rain. Globe News has an exclusive eyewitness account.'

Wobbly video footage of the rain chant appeared on the screen, followed by an interview with Mr Bugwell. Hero choked on his flakes, spluttering them everywhere.

'I saw the Leaford earth warrior start and stop rain with my own eyes,' said Bugwell, smiling at the camera.

Gran was right, thought Hero – Mr Bugwell was the nosiest person in the whole country. Although Dad had previously argued that there was not enough evidence to prove it.

Homes turned to Rivett on the blue sofa in the studio. 'Robin, you're an award-winning reporter; is this story **fact**, **fiction** or just **fantasy**?'

'Yes, I've many awards for my reporting from some of the most dangerous locations in the world. I won

TV Reporter of the Year and have more honorary degrees than I could mention. Although, the award I am most proud of—'

'What about the earth warrior?' interrupted Homes.

'Err … yes … well. It's amazing to see such weather extremes in a short period in Leaford,' grinned Rivett. 'Some say it's global warming, others say it's Leaford's earth warrior. We may never know for sure, but we will do a special investigation over the next few days. I am determined to get to the bottom of it! Wars, conflicts, mass demonstrations and the January sales – Rivett is on the case.'

'Oh no,' muttered Hero. That's all they needed: Rivett poking his nose in and making things worse. Suddenly, Hero's mobile jumped to life with a text from Mitzy telling him to meet her on the Rec as soon as possible.

Hero finished his breakfast and rushed outside - running to the end of the garden, through the back gate and onto the stone bridge. Mitzy and Partha were there already; Partha was standing with hunched shoulders, disguised in a black silk scarf and dark sunglasses.

'What are you doing dressed like that?' snorted Hero.

'We're trespassing,' whispered Partha. 'Those TV

cameras might be around, and I don't want to end up in care. I've borrowed a few things from my Auntie Fatima to make a disguise.' He gave a nervous glance from side to side.

'He's ridiculous,' said Mitzy sharply, 'but let's not waste any more time on him; we've got to find Miss Flowerdew.'

They all crossed the stone bridge and climbed over the broken wooden fence to the Rec.

'I think she's over there,' said Hero, pointing to an abandoned metallic-pink mobility scooter.

They walked along the edge of the riverbank to an area where brambles spilled over rusting, wrought-iron railings. Miss Flowerdew was picking red berries from thorny stems and dropping them into a tatty wicker basket.

'Miss Flowerdew!'

Hero shouted.

Miss Flowerdew turned and peered over her glasses on the tip of her nose, and smiled. 'Have you come to join the protest camp now the rain has stopped?' she said. 'You are most welcome, including your new friend in the sunglasses and scarf.'

'We wanted to ask you a question first,' said Hero,

ignoring Miss Flowerdew's invitation.

'Ask away!' said Miss Flowerdew, smiling.

Mitzy explained that they were looking for the kanna plant for a science project and asked if she knew someone at the botanical gardens.

'What a wonderful assignment!' exclaimed Miss Flowerdew. 'You must go to the botanical gardens and ask for my old friend Mr Prickleswick. Tell him Petula sent you. I'm sure he will be delighted to help you. When you've done your homework, come and join us on the camp. We're expecting quite a crowd.'

'We'll try our best,' lied Hero. He had enough trouble with Dad, never mind getting involved in an illegal trespass.

'Let's get out of here,' muttered Partha, striding off towards the bridge.

No Can Do

'I'm afraid Mr Prickleswick has gone on an expedition to Costa Rica,' said a plump lady. She filled the racing-green wooden ticket office at Leaford's botanical gardens.

'He won't be back for six weeks.'

'Six weeks?' said Hero, wide-eyed. 'We can't wait that long.'

'Can we have three tickets anyway, please?' said Mitzy, pushing in front of Hero.

'Sorry, did you not see the sign?' said the lady. 'We're closed to the public due to flooding of the greenhouses.'

'You mean we're not able to go into any of them?' asked Partha, standing on his tiptoes to peer in the office. 'Not even the African greenhouse?'

The lady grabbed a large packet of beef and onion crisps with fingers crowned with floral-patterned nail extensions. She stuffed the crisps into her mouth and crunched, firing crumbs in all directions. She then took a huge slurp of tea from a mug covered in blue periwinkles.

She completed her mega snack and smacked her lips. 'Sorry, no can do.'

'It's for a school project,' pleaded Mitzy.

'It's a health and safety issue. We should be open again by next week. Return then. Cheerio!'

'That's all we need,' said Hero, crestfallen. As they left the botanical gardens, Hero's mind reeled, thinking what else he could do to get Dad's memory back. They were running out of options.

The air smelled as fresh as clean cotton sheets as Hero and friends walked towards Borromeo Road. The citizens of Leaford had swapped their wellies, raincoats and umbrellas for shorts, T-shirts and sunglasses. They were sitting on benches, chatting, and sunbathing on patches of grass.

'That's strange. Why are so many people on the streets?' said Hero, gazing along the road.

'It's obvious: the sun is back,' replied Mitzy, smiling up at the sunshine.

'But they have backpacks,' said Hero.

Partha and Mitzy surveyed the birch-tree-lined avenue.

A group of lads emerged from a side street laden with rucksacks and rolled-up tents, as if they were going camping.

'Maybe there's an event on,' suggested Partha.

They all arrived at Borromeo Road to find Gran standing at the front door, her face screwed up with worry.

'Hero! I'm so glad to see you,' said Gran in a weak voice. 'Your father has disappeared **AGAIN!**'

Hero looked up to the sky and rolled his eyes. 'He's probably gone fishing.'

Hero led the others through the back gate, across the patch of dusty wasteland and onto the **crumbling** stone bridge. Where he discovered the wooden fence that blocked the entrance to the Rec had been removed.

'Noooooooo waaaaaaaay!'

Hero stood rooted to the spot, his eyes transfixed on the sea of multicoloured tents of varying sizes and shapes that now covered the field. A prickly, uncomfortable feeling spread throughout his body.

'This is where they were all coming,' gasped Partha. 'It's like a music festival.'

There were people talking, singing and mingling. A young couple lay on tartan mats with children running around them. There was an older man and woman sitting on striped deck chairs, students chatting away in a circle. A bearded man played a guitar while a teenager with dreadlocks banged on drums. Some men were bare-chested, wearing loincloths.

Hero scanned the crowd and glimpsed Dad's ostrich feather in the distance. He ran over, squeezing through the wall of bodies to get to him.

'Dad! Err ... TERRA FIRMA!' he yelled.

Dad turned towards Hero, his faced bursting with joy. 'Little Shadow, good to see you,' he said, raising his hands in the air.

'Who are all these people?' asked Hero, being nudged in the back and pushed from side to side.

With a proud, long smile, Dad declared,

'THIS IS MY TRIBE!'

The Tribe

Hero stared up and down at the motley group of scantily clad people. Could this pick-and-mix of old and young, fat and thin, hairy and hairless in an assortment of white, brown and sunburnt red really be Dad's tribe?

'They can't be … I mean, they can't stay here,' said Hero, grimacing at the thought.

'We have set up camp with the help of my warriors, Walking Bear and Barefoot,' said Dad. He raised his hand and beckoned two men to come over.

The first was built like a boulder, with long hair and a black beard and tattoos on both arms. The second was a tall, slim, bronzed athletic man with nothing on his feet. They were both bare-chested and wore chamois-leather loincloths.

'Who are you?' snapped Hero.

'I'm Wayne,' said the bearded man in a deep husky voice.

Dad jerked his head in disapproval.

'BUT … Terra Firma gave me the name Walking Bear. He said I look like a grizzly!'

'I'm Jim,' said the other. 'Terra Firma called me Barefoot because I enjoy running in my bare feet.'

Wow! Dad had never had enough magnetism to attract a paperclip, never mind a tribe. Baggins was right. Dad had become a real sensation.

Mitzy and Partha pushed through the crowd to reach Hero.

'Are all these people here because of your dad?' asked Mitzy, inspecting the horde with a curious delight.

'It looks like it,' replied Hero.

'I told you your dad would be famous,' said Partha excitedly. 'He might even start writing kids' books.'

Hero tried to smile but couldn't quite manage it.

'I knew that TV interview wasn't a good idea,' said Gran, crowding in behind them. 'What is he doing now?'

'He wants to set up camp with his tribe and stay on the Rec,' said Hero.

'Mind yourselves!
Come on!
Make way!' said a familiar voice.

The crowd opened up to show Miss Flowerdew on her metallic-pink mobility scooter.

'Petula!' yelped Gran. 'Are you part of this encampment?'

Miss Flowerdew peered over her yellow glasses. 'Yes, I am. Your Eddie has joined us in our protest.'

'You can't stay here,' objected Hero. 'It's trespassing.'

'All these people are here because of your father's call to save Mother Earth. I don't know what's going on, but it will send a message to the council and Tyranox that we Leafordians will not stand for this!' said Miss Flowerdew.

'Little Shadow, this elder has told us about the threat to Mother Earth from the grey man that digs for gas. We must honour and respect our earth mother,' said Dad.

Hero eyed Gran for support.

'What are you going to do?' asked Mitzy, adjusting her glasses.

'My tribe will take this land for our own, and we will live here in harmony with Mother Earth. If the grey man comes, we will protect her.'

'Good on you, Eddie!' said Miss Flowerdew, punching the air with a fist. 'That's what we need: fighting spirit. We'll not lie down and roll over.'

'Petula is right,' said Gran with a determined nod. 'It's about time we rise up and fight for what we believe in. I'm proud that our Eddie is taking a stand. I've seen Tyranox at work in Nigeria. They're a **NASTY bunch**!'

'Good! I'm glad we're all on the same cabbage patch,' said Miss Flowerdew. 'I must get on. I'm in big demand at the moment.'

Her mobility scooter bleeped as it reversed.

Hero covered his face with his hands and groaned loudly. How could his bookworm dad think he was an earth warrior, create rain, cause flooding and set up a protest camp on the local Rec with his tribe? He had to stop all this craziness straight away before Rivett, Craddock and Slapnatch found out.

Chief Terra Firma

Hero felt uneasy as he watched a hotchpotch of tents form a camp on the Rec. At the top of a long avenue of coloured canvases, there was the main campfire – a circle of grey stones taken from the crumbling bridge with a pile of wood in the middle. Further back from the campfire was a large round red and white candy-striped marquee with two smaller oval tents with scalloped edging on each side.

Tribe members had been busy all day like ants on their new land, digging and planting seeds in areas marked for growing food. Some went fishing in the River Leaf, hunted rabbits and pigeons in the undergrowth or practised shooting arrows and throwing homemade spears at targets. Others picked wild berries and cooked on small stoves near their tents.

Hero couldn't believe Leaford Rec, which used to be home to dog walkers, runners and kids playing football, had now been transformed into a tribal camp.

As the sky turned copper orange and a light chill replaced the heat of the day, Hero joined Gran, Mitzy and Partha and the tribe members around the campfire. A couple with dreadlocks beat brown and white animal-skin drums while everyone chanted.

The drumming suddenly stopped. Silence descended on the camp with the usual exception of a beeping mobile, a dog barking and a baby crying. Dad came out of his tent wearing his ostrich-feathered headscarf and a variety of multicoloured gemstone-beaded necklaces of turquoise, coral, ruby and lapis. A green diamond-patterned cloth was wrapped tightly round his waist.

Hero wondered if someone had got Dad's new outfit from Spirit and Spice on Leaford market. Wherever it came from, he certainly looked the part.

Dad bowed his head and spoke, as the rest of the tribe listened.

'Oh, Mother Earth, whose voice sings in the wind, whose breath gives life to all the world, hear us. We are small and weak. We need your strength and wisdom.'

**'Whaa woo woo woo!
Whaa woo woo woo!'**

shouted the tribe members.

Dad stood upright, his chin raised in the air, his face proud and resolute.

'RESPECT MOTHER EARTH!'

**'Whaa woo woo woo!
Whaa woo woo woo!'**

'RESPECT THE WEB OF LIFE!'

**'Whaa woo woo woo!
Whaa woo woo woo!'**

'RESPECT THE AIR WE BREATHE, THE WATER WE DRINK, THE FOOD WE EAT!'

**'Whaa woo woo woo!
Whaa woo woo woo!'**

As the chanting of the tribe faded, Hero could make out muffled sounds from behind. The sound got louder and louder until everyone turned around to see what the commotion was all about. The crowd parted to reveal Chief Inspector Craddock, Slapnatch and a bald, stocky man with a ginger goatee wearing a black suit.

'Are you aware that you're trespassing?' said the chief inspector with a disapproving stare. 'This area is no longer for public use and is owned by **Tyranox Energy**.'

Hero shrunk in height and side-stepped closer to Gran.

'Mr Barnabas Vump is the president of Tyranox and the rightful owner of this land,' snapped the stocky, bald man in a strong accent. 'You are all trespassers!'

'Who's he?' muttered Hero, not liking the look of him.

'Which tribe are you?' asked Dad.

'I'm Dimitri, Vump's executive assistant,' snarled the man. 'You need to leave immediately.'

'My tribe has taken this land to protect Mother Earth,' said Dad.

'Ha! Protect Mother Earth?' sneered Slapnatch.

'The man is deranged. We need to protect the boy.'

He grinned at Hero, licking his lips as if he were eyeing prey. Hero's heart quickened.

'No! I ain't going anywhere,' he yelled.

'We'll soon see about that,' said Slapnatch.

'Tyranox will drop all charges for trespassing if you vacate this land,' said Inspector Craddock, looking towards the bald man for approval.

'The Rec is owned by the people of Leaford,' shouted Miss Flowerdew from her mobility scooter. 'The chief councillor had no right to sell off our green space.'

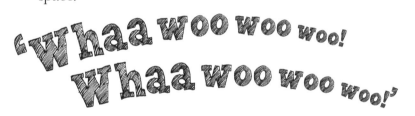

cried the tribe members.

'If you are not willing to leave, then I must insist on taking the boy with us now,' said the chief inspector as sweat cascaded down his face.

Slapnatch nodded, grinned and bounded forward to take Hero.

'The boy ain't going anywhere,' said Walking Bear, moving in front of Hero.

'This is unacceptable!' said Inspector Craddock. 'If you do not get off this land within twenty-four hours, I will forcibly remove you.'

Hero hid behind Walking Bear and poked his tongue out at Slapnatch, who was now red with rage.

'You've been warned!' said Dimitri. 'We know how to deal with people like you.'

'Your bully tactics won't work here,' yelled Gran. 'We Leafordians are made of strong stuff!'

'They're clearly not going to move,' said Inspector Craddock. 'We need reinforcements. Come on, let's go.'

Dimitri shot a daggered glance over his shoulder at Gran and snarled. 'You'll be sorry, wait and see,' he muttered as he marched off.

sounded the camera of the *Bugle*'s photographer.

Reporter Jameel Jawar scribbled away on his notepad. 'Did the man from Tyranox threaten you?' he asked.

Dad nodded. 'We need to be tolerant of those who have lost their way.'

'Do you intend to vacate the Rec, Terra Firma?' said Jawar, scratching his brown beard.

'First, I must talk with the chief who has sold the land that the people walk on,' returned Dad.

'Would you be willing to have the *Leaford Bugle* cover the story if we get Chief Councillor Erik Onions to meet with you?' said Jawar, sniffing a scoop.

'No!' said Hero, disapprovingly. 'All this publicity got you into this situation.'

'You'll meet with the chief sooner rather than later,' chimed in Walking Bear.

'You need to leave the Rec; otherwise you'll be arrested,' said Hero, distrustful of the local newspaper getting involved.

'Bring the chief of the council here tomorrow at noon,' said Dad.

'He'll just make things worse,' said Hero, his spirits plummeting.

'Little Shadow, we need to speak,' said Dad. 'Only by talking can we resolve conflict and restore harmony.'

Hero stared at Mitzy and Partha. 'We've got to try that truth serum straight away,' he whispered. 'It's our only chance now to stop Dad from going to prison and me into care.'

'Don't worry,' said Mitzy with a new confidence in her voice. 'I've an idea where we might just find what we're looking for. Come on, Partha. We have work to do!'

Chief to Chief

The next day at noon, the sun hung like a golden disc in the aqua-blue sky. Tribe members gathered round the stone-ringed campfire as drums, flutes and song provided the mood music for the meeting of the chiefs.

Hero stood with Gran at the end of the long avenue of tents, his fingers and toes tingling at the prospect of coming face to face with the man who had disrupted his football playing: Chief Councillor Onions.

An oversized figure wobbled across the Rec with three grey-suited figures following behind like obedient dogs. Chief Councillor Onions arrived panting, wiping beads of sweat from his balding head.

Hero watched Dad greet the delegation, posing for a photo and shaking hands with Onions. He then followed the group into a large striped marquee.

There were the reporter Jameel Jawar, Walking Bear, Barefoot, Gran, Onions and his grey assistants.

'Welcome to my camp,' said Dad, staring into Onions's eyes.

'I am pleased to meet you too,' said Onions. 'But not when you're trespassing.'

'It is the wish of my people to live here. We must protect this land and respect Mother Earth, who has nurtured us like a baby,' replied Dad in a solemn tone.

'This is an unauthorised and illegal camp. You need to vacate the Rec now!' said Onions, screwing up his nose in disgust.

'Chief of the Council, I ask you to stop this destruction of Mother Earth and let us stay here.'

'I cannot do that. The Rec belongs to Tyranox.'

Hero's body tensed, and a surge of heat rushed to his head. 'We've got nowhere to play football because of you,' he said brusquely.

'There are lots of places where you can do that,' said Onions. 'Selling the Rec will improve vital services and help create jobs for the people of Leaford.'

'It's the only green space for miles,' returned Hero. 'You sold off the playing fields near our school to the supermarket.'

'We had no choice.' Onions pulled out his polka-dot handkerchief and patted his brow dry.

'I can't believe you did it,' added Hero, disappointed.

'It was a democratic decision. The councillors, elected by the residents of Leaford, voted for this. We can't stop the will of the people!'

'A chief must listen to his people … That is right,' said Dad, nodding in agreement.

For a moment, Hero feared Dad was coming round to Onions's way of thinking, especially if everyone in Leaford agreed with the fracking.

Dad eyed Onions. 'But we do not own this land but borrow it from our children. We therefore must protect it so they can enjoy it as we do now.'

'I ask you again to leave this Rec,' growled the chief councillor.

Suddenly, Dad moved closer to Onions and placed his hands above his fat head.

'I'll have you arrested if you touch me,' said Onions, cowering.

Dad closed his eyes and quivered his fingers as if he were touching something.

Hero stared, baffled by Dad's behaviour.

Dad frowned, concentrating. 'I feel a severe blockage in your chakras.'

'Enough of this nonsense!'

yelled Onions, moving away from Dad. 'I ask you again to leave this land. If not, you will be removed.'

Dad gave a disappointed stare. 'Your smooth language can make right look wrong and wrong look right. But this will always be wrong.'

'I'm afraid, according to the law, this is right. Now the sooner you vacate the Rec, the better,' growled Onions. 'I have nothing more to say.'

With that, Councillor Onions exited the marquee to disapproving jeers from the tribe members.

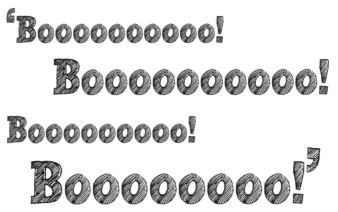

'Booooooooooo! Boooooooooooo! Booooooooo! Boooooooooo!'

Dad stared ahead in thought. 'As sure as the great bear searches for the sweet honey,' he said earnestly, 'the chief will return with his grey men.'

Hero looked at Dad. 'We need to leave the Rec.'

'We need to fight,' said Dad, determined.

Hero blinked, swallowed hard and croaked,

'**FIGHT?** But you said speaking creates harmony.'

Dad tilted his head and looked at Hero. 'Sometimes balance is only restored after chaos. We must fight for what we believe.'

'You're right, Eddie,' said Gran, frowning. 'We can't let that big lump ruin our community. Tell the tribe to bring old wood, furniture … anything to build a barricade.'

'Gran! What are you saying?' protested Hero. 'Dad will be arrested.'

'Don't worry, dear. Things have a way of sorting themselves out.'

Hero bit his lip in frustration.

'Well, I'd better get back; I need to pack some essentials. Once the barrier goes up, we could be here for the duration. I'll see you in the morning,' said Gran, hurrying out of the tent.

screamed Hero. 'This heat is turning everyone bonkers!'

Prepare for Battle

That night, Hero tossed and turned in the tent, trying to sleep. The floor was hard and rough like a walnut, but Hero wasn't bothered about that – his mind was occupied by the impending confrontation with the police.

He longed to get his old dad back. He wouldn't care if he spent all his time reading his encyclopaedias – at least he'd know where he was. As for going to see the World Cup, well that wouldn't be possible now. He gave a heavy sigh, ignoring the turmoil inside. He then placed his forehead on his arm and squeezed his eyes tight, trying to escape into sleep.

The next morning, Hero was awoken by Walking Bear, wearing an orange headband and multicoloured beads. His hairy body was painted red, yellow and blue.

'Little Shadow, come and prepare yourself for battle,' he said.

Half asleep, Hero dragged himself to his feet and left the tent for the dazzling morning sunshine.

'Wow!' he said, not believing his sleepy eyes.

Outside there was a group of bare-chested warriors gathered in a circle painting zigzags on their foreheads, and arrows, diamonds and whorls on their bodies. It wasn't long before his own body was being covered in red paint too.

'This colour symbolises strength and success in battle,' said Walking Bear as Barefoot painted Hero's face. Next came a black zigzag line on his forehead.

'This line symbolises lightning, which will give you power and speed.'

Hero ate a hearty breakfast of free-range eggs, veggie-sausages and beans that had been cooked on a camp stove. Then, covered in paint and feeling rather silly, he joined the other warriors in a circle round the stone-ringed campfire.

Dad came out of the marquee wearing his ostrich-feathered headscarf and mustard chamois-leather loincloth. He had red, yellow and blue stripes painted on each cheek and whorls and diamonds on his body.

BOOM! BOOM! BOOM!

went the drums.

'**Yoooooooo!**' replied the warriors all together.

Dad raised his hand in the air. The drumming stopped, and the warriors stood still, waiting for their chief to speak.

'Today we fight,' he said in a defiant voice.

'**Yoooooooo!**' screamed the tribe members, shaking their homemade weaponry in the air.

'We fight so we can sit on this ground.'

'**Yoooooooo!**'

'We fight so we can touch this soil.'

'**Yoooooooo!**'

'We fight to protect Mother Earth!'

'**Yoooooooo!**'

'We fight so our children can live in harmony!'

'Yooooooooo!'

'We fight because we are **EARTH WARRIORS**!'

Dad thrust his brush-handled spear in the air, causing the tribe to go crazy.

'Yooooooooo! Yooooooooo!'

'Yooooooooo! Yooooooooo!'

Fear gripped Hero. *This is not good, not good at all,* he thought. He yearned for Gran to come back and stop all this madness.

TING-A-LING! TING-A-LING!

People turned around one by one. The noise subsided until old Mr Percy appeared, dressed in a green safari hat, a dirty string vest and shorts. He shook a large dull brass bell while leaning on a wooden walking stick.

'They're here!' he croaked. 'Our time has come. Take your places to fight for our land!'

Rivett's Retreat

Hero stared through the barricade at a well-groomed Rivett in his electric-blue tailored suit and burgundy tie. He stood facing the camera in front of a mountain of old chairs, wood, fences and metal tubes that blocked the main entrance to the Rec.

'Alistair, whether it's war zones or troubled hotspots, I am once again here where it matters, endangering my life to bring minute-by-minute news coverage of unfolding events,' beamed Rivett.

'Yes, but please tell our patient viewers where you are and what is going on,' said Homes, through gritted teeth.

'Well, I'm here at the Leaford Rec, where five hundred people have barricaded themselves on the site. They're refusing to move after talks with Chief Councillor Erik Onions broke down yesterday,' said Rivett.

The clatter and clash of objects could be heard in the background.

'The illegal occupation is being led by Leaford Council employee Eddie Trough, now turned earth warrior, who is protesting at Tyranox's plans to drill for gas. The police have been notified and are taking out an eviction order.'

'We're not moving!' shouted tribe members. 'This is our field. If you frack, you can't go back! No fracking in Leaford!'

SPLAT, SPLASH, SPLAT, SPLASH, SPLAT, SPLASH!

Balloon water bombs rained down from the top of the barricade.

'Ouch! Heeee! Noo!' cried Rivett.

Homemade darts blown through straws hit him on the backside.

'ARGGH! That hurt!'

With his hair and electric-blue suit drenched, the patch-eyed award-winning reporter abandoned his broadcast, leaving Homes and thousands of viewers bemused.

*

Hero sat on the ragged remains of an old armchair. He placed his elbows on his knees and his face in his hands, thinking. He had to find Gran and persuade her to stop the protest before Dad got arrested. But where was she? She said she would be back in the morning, but she was nowhere to be seen.

He stood up and hurried towards the side of the barricade, where he squeezed through a small gap in the pile of discarded objects – which included old wood, doors, wardrobes and a park bench.

Hunched up and knees bent in order not to be seen, he scurried across the dusty wasteland to 32 Borromeo Road. There he dashed down the back garden, only to find the kitchen door locked. He rapped hard but there was no answer.

Hero ran to the front of the house to see if Gran was upstairs. He banged on the red front door several times before shouting through the tarnished brass letterbox.

'Gran! Are you there? It's me,' Hero yelled.

'You won't need your gran where you're going,' said a sinister, squeaky voice.

Hero turned to find Slapnatch standing there, his nose crinkled into a long reddish snout, with a grin so large it exposed his yellowish, rat-like teeth. Hero darted away from the front door, dodging Slapnatch's attempts to grab him, escaping to the side of the house and into the garden.

He eyed the gate that led to the Rec. But before he could pelt it down the dry lawn, a hairy arm as hard as concrete grabbed him and pulled him back.

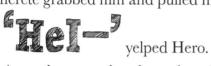 yelped Hero.

A rough, sweaty hand smothered his face.

Slapnatch appeared, smirking.

'Good job, Reggie,' he said. 'Our plan went like clockwork.'

Hero struggled as Slapnatch moved closer.

'So you thought you would get away, eh? No kid escapes from Slapnatch!' He nibbled his bottom lip with his protruding teeth.

Hero cried for help but his call was muffled. He couldn't move, restrained by his captor.

'My dear friend Miss Callous will look after you,' said Slapnatch, flattening his greasy hair with his long fingers. 'That'll put an end to this protest. Onions will be happy, and I'll get my promotion to head of social services.'

Hero's eyes widened and his face burned as he struggled to breathe.

'Easy, Reggie. We must protect this vulnerable specimen,' grinned Slapnatch.

The hand loosened, allowing Hero to catch his breath. He inhaled, opening his mouth wide to call for help, but before he could do so, several porky fingers crossed his lips.

Hero bit hard into what felt like a stone-sausage sandwich. The grip weakened. He kicked backwards against Reggie's leg, first one heel and then the other. Before he knew it, Hero was sprinting towards the back gate.

Suddenly a muscular man with the face of a bulldog leaped from behind the shed, blocking his path.

Hero skidded to a halt.

'Ronnie! Get him,'

yelled Slapnatch to Reggie's twin brother.

Hero glanced over his shoulder to see that his captors were in close pursuit.

He was trapped.

Scanning the garden in desperation, he caught sight of his football beside the fence. He ran and whacked it into the air.

The ball flew upwards before hitting Ronnie hard in the face.

The man collapsed.

'Get up, you useless lump!' squealed Slapnatch.

Reggie lurched forward to grab the boy. But Hero was too fast, and the brute tripped over and crashed to the ground.

Hero was free at last.

Voice of Truth

Hero returned to the safety of the camp, panting like a dehydrated hyena. He wiped the sweat from his flushed face and guzzled down several cups of water. He had had a lucky escape, but he still needed to find Gran.

After taking a rest inside the tent, he left and headed for the main barricade. He walked through the crowd and caught sight of Mitzy and Partha climbing over a pile of furniture at the side of the Rec.

'Don't just stand there. **Help me!**' yelled Mitzy, standing on an old sofa.

Hero held out his hands. Mitzy took hold of them and jumped down.

'**I'm stuck!**' squeaked Partha, as he tried to scramble over a broken wooden door.

'Your scarf is caught on a nail,' said Mitzy, releasing

him. 'I told you it's a silly disguise.'

Partha climbed down and smirked at Hero.

'Why do you look like a multicoloured Dalmatian? Have you joined the circus?'

Hero glanced down at his body; the war paint was smudged into blotches of colour.

'We tried Mystic Martin's Emporium in town, but it was closed,' said Mitzy matter-of-factly.

Hero stared vacantly at Mitzy. With Rivett turning up and then nearly being snatched by Slapnatch, he had forgotten all about the truth serum.

'It wouldn't have worked anyway,' he said, with disappointment written all over his face.

'We went to the bakery next door,' said Partha excitedly. 'They have the largest selection of cakes in the whole of Leaford! Jam tarts, vanilla slices, egg custards, chocolate eclairs, raspberry ripple cupcakes and—'

'But no truth serum.'

'What Partha wanted to say – before he got distracted by his sweet tooth – is that the man at the bakery told us that Mystic Martin closed the shop to join the camp,' said Mitzy.

'It doesn't matter now. There's no way we'll find him in this lot. We don't even know what he looks like,' said Hero, kicking a dried-up lump of soil.

'BUT …' said Mitzy, cocking her head and curling her top lip, 'Mystic Martin left the key with the man at the bakery, who, after I told him what we wanted, was kind enough to get it for us.'

She waved her hand in the air with all the panache of a magician lifting a white rabbit out of a black hat, to reveal a small blue glass bottle with a golden swirled top.

'You've got it!' said Hero, wide-eyed.

'FANTASTIC!'

The bottle had a brown label with VOICE OF TRUTH written on it in old-fashioned lettering.

'I've water and reusable cups in my backpack,' said Mitzy, pointing to the strap on her shoulder. 'All we need to do is give your dad the serum.'

'Come on, let's find him,' said Hero, bounding forward. 'We can start over there.'

But before they could begin their search for Dad, a voice yelled

'STOP!
STOP!'

Hero turned to see the burning, sweaty face of Mr Bugwell.

'It's your gran,' he gasped. 'She's been taken.'

'Taken…? By who? The police?' said Hero.

Mr Bugwell panted heavily before taking in a deep breath. 'No, she's been **KIDNAPPED**!' he wheezed, his chest collapsing like a deflated balloon.

Bugwell's Theory

Hero and the others retreated from the heat into Dad's marquee, keen to find out what Bugwell was talking about.

'That's better!' said Bugwell, after drinking several cups of water.

'Where is Gran?' said Hero impatiently.

Bugwell grinned like a monkey in a banana warehouse. 'I can answer that question,' he said, taking out a spiral-ringed notebook from the pocket of his shorts.

'At 7.35, Mrs Rosangela Trough was seen in the shed in the rear garden of number 32 Borromeo Road. A little while later, at 8.10, a white van pulled up at the front of the house. Two stocky men dressed in green overalls got out and proceeded down the path.'

Mr Bugwell stopped and turned a page.

'The two men took Mrs Trough senior against her will. She protested and struggled before being flung into the back of their vehicle.'

'Why didn't you call the police or shout for help?' said Hero with an increased pitch in his voice.

'I called them but they're all tied up. What with the flooding and the protest camp, I wasn't sure how long they would be, so I thought I'd better inform you myself. I've been looking for you everywhere!'

Hero scratched his head. 'Why would anyone want to kidnap Gran? Where would they take her?'

'Perhaps I could shed light on the matter,' said Mr Bugwell. 'With my Superissimo binoculars – they're the highest magnitude on the market, you know – I was able to see inside the back of the van. I saw that there was a board with **KEEP OUT** written on it.'

'How can that help us?' said Hero, his body tensing.

'Well, the sign was the same one that had been put on the gate of Leaford Rec.'

'Aren't all these signs the same?' said Partha, adjusting the silk scarf round his neck.

'Tyranox was printed in **bold** red letters!' replied Bugwell.

'You mean someone from Tyranox kidnapped

Gran?' Hero played through the implications of what Bugwell had said.

'It's one theory. If you wanted Eddie to leave the Rec, then this is a way of doing it.'

'I'm not convinced,' said Hero. 'It could be the guy who put the sign up, not Tyranox.'

'They would still work for them!' exclaimed Mr Bugwell.

'If your theory is true,' said Mitzy cautiously, 'where would they have taken her?'

'I can help you there too!' said Mr Bugwell, smiling and twirling the end of his small moustache. 'Tyranox has a works depot on the old Ramsbottom chocolate factory site on the edge of Leaford. It was mentioned in the *Bugle* a while back. I bet she's there.'

Hero persuaded Mr Bugwell to rest in another tent to avoid getting sunstroke. This provided an opportunity for him to discuss the new development with his friends, away from his nosy neighbour.

'We've got to find out if this is true,' said Hero, pacing up and down inside the marquee. 'I didn't like the look of that Dimitri man. I bet he's involved in this.'

Partha laughed. 'You can't say he's kidnapped your gran just because you weren't keen on him.'

'You're right, but I don't trust him,' said Hero. 'There's only one thing we can do now: we've got to find Gran.'

'But what about your dad and the truth serum?' asked Mitzy.

Hero munched on his lip, thinking hard. 'I need Terra Firma to help rescue Gran; Dad would be useless in such a situation.'

'So, what are you saying? You want your dad to remain a warrior?'

'If it means saving Gran, then **YES!**'

'And the truth serum?' said Partha with a frown.'We've wasted nearly a whole day looking for it.'

'Keep it safe, just in case we need it later,' said Hero. 'Now come on, we need to find Dad.'

Warrior Spirit

Hero stood on his toes, stretched his neck and peered over the crowd that had gathered around the barricade. Catching sight of Dad's rainbow headscarf and white ostrich feather, he weaved through the warm wall of bodies to reach him.

'Dad ... err ... Terra Firma!' exclaimed Hero. 'Gran ... err ... Fire Bird ... has been kidnapped.'

'We know the news you bring, Little Shadow,' said Dad in a soft voice.

'How?'

Walking Bear marched forward waving a printed piece of paper in the air. 'This letter was left at the barricade,' he said. 'They say they will harm Fire Bird if we do not leave this land.'

'It's terrible!' yelled Miss Flowerdew from

her mobility scooter. 'They're not playing fair.'

'Mr Bugwell thinks she's been taken to the old Ramsbottom chocolate factory,' said Hero, eager to do something to find Gran.

Dad gazed at Miss Flowerdew. 'Elder, how do we get to this place?'

'Now, let me see,' she said, removing her battered straw hat and scratching her untamed grey wiry hair. 'Well, the police will patrol the main route into the centre. It'll take too long to go around the city. So, the only direct way to the old Ramsbottom site is by the river.'

'The river?' asked Hero. 'But we don't have a boat.'

'Two tribe members have brought canoes. We can use them,' informed Walking Bear.

'I will rescue Fire Bird,' said Dad. 'For she is in danger because of me.'

'You can't do it alone,' said Walking Bear in a warning voice. 'It would be suicide.'

'Mother Earth will be with me. She will give me the strength of the bear, the cunning of the coyote and the swiftness of the eagle.'

An overpowering urge took control of Hero, and before he knew it, he blurted, **'I want to come!'**

'No!' snapped Walking Bear, his beard bristling in protest. 'It's dangerous, you'll get hurt.'

Dad looked Walking Bear in the eye. 'My friend, there is a time when the spirit of the true warrior inside must reveal itself,' he said calmly. 'When that time comes, do not fear it or let it pass you by. But embrace it, tame it like a wild stallion and become its master.'

He turned to Hero. 'Little Shadow, you have a strong will to rescue Fire Bird. Together we will find Fire Bird and bring her home. You may leave as a boy, but you will return a man.'

Hero grinned nervously, his heart beating fast.

At that moment, Barefoot appeared. 'The chief inspector is here. He wants to speak with you.'

Hero watched Dad climb up onto the barricade with his homemade spear in his hand. Below stood Chief Inspector Craddock, surrounded by ten police officers.

'I will ask you again,' said the chief inspector, squinting at the tall, slim and newly tanned figure of Dad in the sunlight. 'Leave this site or I will remove you, and that would be nasty.'

'This land is our home,' replied Dad defiantly. 'We will not leave.'

'Right then, I've no choice,' said the chief inspector. He waved his hand, signalling to the officers to dismantle the barricade. 'Let's get rid of these blighters!'

Hero sensed things were spiralling out of control.

'**BOOOooooooooooooooooooooooooooo!** Leave us in peace,' cried the tribe members as the officers removed pieces of wood, chairs and metal fencing. 'You are the criminals!' they yelled.

Water bombs –

'**OOUUUUCH!**'

– homemade arrows –

'**AARRRGGH!**'

– stones –

BASH!

– and Frisbees rained down on the police officers until they couldn't stand it any more and started a retreat.

'**Yeaaaaah!**'  cried the tribe members.

'Phew!' said Hero, relieved the police were finally going. Dad turned to Walking Bear and Barefoot and placed his hands firmly on their shoulders. 'Our time has come, my warriors. Be prepared to fight. Be prepared to die. Be prepared for war!'

 yelped Hero, horrified.

Hero waited outside Dad's marquee with his eyes closed, feeling the warm sunshine on his skin. As he reflected on his situation, he heard Mum's voice in his head, 'Be the change you want to see.'

But how could he change anything now?

After a few minutes of thinking, though, he had a plan. He first must rescue Gran; then, he would deal with the protest and get Dad's memory back.

His train of thought was broken by the sound of someone moving closer. He opened his eyes to find Mr Bugwell standing in front of him wearing a straw panama hat and dark sunglasses.

'Have you decided what you will do about your gran?' he said nosily.

'Err … hmmm …' said Hero, unsure whether to tell the truth or not. 'Me and Dad are going to rescue her.'

'How?' said Mr Bugwell, looking at him, utterly incredulous. 'We're surrounded.'

'Down the river in a canoe.'

'You're mad! Has your father ever canoed down a turbulent river?'

A sudden **Shiver** of alarm spread over Hero. Dad had never used a canoe in his life.

At that moment, Dad appeared. 'Come, Little Shadow,' he said, marching off. 'Let us find Fire Bird and bring her home.'

The Rescue

Hero stared at the surging white river water as the canoe strained at its tether. He felt his stomach fizz with nervous anticipation.

'Little Shadow, do you fear water?' asked Dad.

'Err ... no ... but the river is high ... and flowing fast,' replied Hero in a weak voice. 'Are you sure it's safe? We could drown.'

'Do not hide from that which you fear,' said Dad solemnly. 'You must live your life with courage in your heart.'

Hero scowled, not understanding what Dad meant.

Dad had misjudged his footing climbing into the canoe and had fallen straight into the river. Hero bent down, grabbed Dad by the arm and pulled him onto the boat.

'**OOOOOOHH!** The water is fresh,' shuddered Dad.

Hero wondered whether it was such a good idea to go in a canoe to rescue Gran after all. But before another doubtful thought could take shape, they were being transported down the river.

Hero glanced longingly at the camp with its mosaic of coloured tents, and caught sight of Mitzy and Partha jumping up and down waving. He gave a half-hearted wave back before taking a paddle.

The flooded river had engulfed the trees on its bank. Bare white branches stuck up into the air like ghostly arms crying for help. Dad sat in the front of the canoe, guiding it past the many obstacles they encountered.

'Mother Earth will be pleased by your bravery, Little Shadow. She is proud of me now I am a chief and have a tribe of warriors to protect her.'

Dad stared ahead as he paddled through the turbulent water.

'But do not fear. We'll soon rescue your mother.'

'What?' exclaimed Hero, not quite believing his ears. 'My mum's dead.'

There was a long pause. Then Dad said, 'That pains my heart to hear what you say. A brain tumour is a terrible disease.'

Hero glared, confused by Dad's words.

'How do you know?' said Hero, tensing his jaw.

'She was my wife.'

Dad placed his hand on the side of his head.

'Dad … Terra Firma. W-what's wrong?' stuttered Hero.

Dad mumbled.

Hero touched Dad's shoulder. His body flopped forward.

'Dad, come on!'

Dad grunted.

Hero squeezed past Dad to the front of the canoe and grabbed the wooden paddle. He pushed Dad backwards so he was lying on his back with his knees bent.

The river was suddenly an assault course with rocks, branches and pieces of tree trunk racing along it. Hero's heart thudded in his chest as he tried to keep afloat.

'Wake up! Wake up!' he yelled.

But Dad lay still.

Hero's stomach wobbled and settled as the canoe became more agitated.

'Dad, please!' cried Hero in desperation.

'Grrrr … What?' said Dad, opening his eyes and rubbing his head. 'Hero … where … are we?'

'Dad?' asked Hero.

Dad's voice was different. Hero glanced fleetingly over his shoulder. Under the layer of smudged paint, Dad's face had changed too. He had lost that stern, proud expression.

'Terra Firma?' said Hero in a timid tone.

'What?' replied Dad.

'Err … I can't explain now,' said Hero.

'Where are my clothes? Who's painted my body? Why do I look like Tarzan? Have I been to a fancy dress?'

'Gran has been kidnapped,' said Hero, realising Dad was back. 'We're going to rescue her.'

Dad squeezed his eyebrows together, making the line between them more prominent.

'Is this one of those role-playing games I have read about?'

'NO! Gran is in danger,' barked Hero as he avoided another rock.

'Don't tell me I'm dreaming,' said Dad, scratching his head.

'DAD! You're not. Please take the paddle,' yelled Hero. 'This is **REAL**!'

'No, I don't believe it. My nose says it's real; my skin says it's real; my eyes say it's real; and my ears say it's real. But my brain doesn't. This is a dream and I will stop it now!' said Dad, standing up in protest.

The canoe jolted along the river as Dad tried to keep his balance.

'Mind your head!' yelled Hero.

A low-hanging branch hit Dad's head. He fell down into the boat.

'Dad! Are you okay?' said Hero.

There was no answer.

Hero returned his gaze to the front of the canoe, his eyes bulging at the sight of what lay ahead. For the canoe was being pulled towards a weir where the water cascaded, fast and furious.

With all his might, Hero gripped the wooden paddle until his fingers burned. But the force of the water was too much. His guts twisted with fear as the canoe sped out of control to the edge of the weir.

'NOoooooooooooo!'

With its monstrous strength, the river flung the canoe over the weir, shaking it from side to side, spinning it upside down and plunging Hero into its gurgling depths.

Hero gasped for air as cool water engulfed his body. He pushed out his arms, kicking his legs to stay afloat, his heart galloping. But the turbulence was too much and swept him away with the debris.

He caught sight of a log approaching fast. Stretching out one arm he grabbed a small branch and pulled himself towards it. This allowed him to grip the trunk with both hands and hug it for dear life.

The log transported Hero down the river, jumping

and jolting in protest. When the water became calmer, the wood was flung to the bank. It was as if the river had got bored and no longer wanted to play. This gave Hero the opportunity to crawl to safety.

He gulped, taking in deep breaths, tasting the strong smell of vegetation that filled the air.

He had survived. But where was Dad?

Dr A. B. C.

'Daaaaaaaaaaad!!!'

A wave of terror ripped through Hero's body at the thought that Dad might have drowned. His heart pounded against his ribcage, the thud echoing in his head. He squeezed his eyes to hold back the tears. He couldn't give up. He had to find Dad. He swallowed hard and took in a deep breath, walking along the riverbank. Catching sight of something in the distance, he hurried towards it, only to discover it was an old tree trunk.

Hero continued searching until he came across a shape amongst the mud and vegetation. He ran to investigate, his feet sinking and squelching with each step.

It was the wet, muddy figure of Dad.

"Dad!" yelled Hero. He grabbed Dad's limp body, tugged him over onto his back and pulled him up from the river.

'Dad, are you okay?' He gasped at the sight of Dad's expressionless, mud-splattered face.

There was no answer.

He bit his lip, wondering how to deal with his dilemma, for they were miles away from anywhere.

It was then that 'Dr A. B. C.' pierced his consciousness. That's what Dad had always told him he should do in an emergency:

D - DANGER

R - RESPONSE

A - AIRWAYS

B - BREATHING

C - CARDIAC

Hero looked around to ensure Dad was safe.

'Dad! Can you hear me?' he said.

Nothing.

He lifted Dad's chin upwards so his head was tilted back to open his airways. Dad didn't seem to be breathing. Hero lowered his head onto Dad's chest, but there was no heartbeat.

He stared at Dad, trying hard to remember. Like bits of a jigsaw puzzle, piece by piece the things Dad had taught him about first aid returned to form a picture in his mind.

Hero took the tip of Dad's nose between two of his fingers with his left hand. He then placed the fingertips of his right hand onto Dad's chin, pulling his nose backwards and chin forward to open his mouth. Hero took a large breath and lowered his head to press his mouth against Dad's, but he couldn't do it. He set his breath free. Finding the courage to try again, he took an even deeper breath and then put his lips to Dad's, releasing the air into his mouth. He did this three times, watching to see if his chest moved.

He wasn't sure.

Hero strained his brow to recall the chest compressions Dad had taught him to the tune of 'Nelly the Elephant'. He placed one hand on top of the other, spreading the fingers of the lower hand in the middle of Dad's ribcage, and pressed down hard.

'Nelly!' he cried. But before he could speak another word, Dad sprung to life, gasping for air. He turned to his side, coughing. Water spurted out of his nose and mouth as his chest rose and fell like a piston on an engine, taking in more air. Dad groaned before opening his eyes.

'Dad!' cried Hero, relieved he was alive. 'Are you all right?' he said, helping him to sit up.

'I'm fine, son,' replied Dad in a raspy voice.

After about an hour, Dad seemed somewhat better. He complained that his body ached, and he still wobbled when he tried to walk, but the worst had passed. Hero filled him in on what had happened.

'I cannot comprehend this,' said Dad, his forehead creased like a folded newspaper. 'It's totally illogical.'

'Weird for me too,' said Hero, 'but we have to find Gran.'

'No, the best thing is to call the police,' said Dad adamantly. 'This is not some game, Hero.'

'If you do that, you will be arrested,' said Hero, wide-eyed. 'They won't believe you, and it could be too late for Gran.'

Dad crumpled his face and touched the side of his head.

'I appreciate that under my psychotic state, my deportment may be misconstrued to have transgressed the laws of civility.'

'Are you sure you're all right?' asked Hero, leaning forward to inspect Dad's face.

'It might take time before I'm compos mentis. Now, where were we?'

'We have to rescue Gran. Mr Bugwell said she's in danger.'

'Mr Bugwell?' asked Dad, grabbing his hair with one hand.

'He's our neighbour, remember?'

'Bugwell? Oh … yes, it's coming back. He's not known for his precision and accuracy, is he?'

'What are we going to do about Gran?' said Hero, unsure whether his dad was really all right.

'We will prove, or perhaps disprove, your hypothesis that Gran is in danger. To do this, we need to find her.'

Hero shook his head wearily.

'I may be suffering from synapse lapse,' said Dad, touching his temples.

'What's that?' enquired Hero.

'A delay in the transmission of information between

brain cells. You'll have to help me fill in the gaps if I can't remember.'

'I will, but let's get a move on,' said Hero. 'The old Ramsbottom factory shouldn't be that far.'

They started to walk, but after a few minutes, Dad came to a standstill.

Hero scowled at Dad. 'What is it?'

Dad looked down at his muddy bare feet. 'I've lost my flip-flops!'

'Try to stay on the path,' said Hero, tensing his jaw. 'Come on, we've got to get going.'

As they walked along the riverbank, Hero gave a deep sigh of relief. Dad had been found alive. Now they had to rescue Gran – but first, they had to find her.

Tarzan Physics

Hero surveyed the fields along the riverbank. 'We've been walking for ages. It must be around here somewhere. Is that it over there?' he said, pointing to a tall grey corrugated-metal building in the distance.

Dad squinted and scratched his head. 'Yes ... I remember now. That's the remains of the old Ramsbottom chocolate factory. It's been closed for over a decade – a victim of globalisation.'

'I hope Mr Bugwell is right about Gran being there,' said Hero. 'Otherwise this will be a total waste of time.'

'It is plausible. If I recall, it's the largest vacant site in Leaford,' Dad replied.

They walked further along the riverbank through the dried vegetation towards the old chocolate factory.

'Wasn't Cecil Ramsbottom a philanthropist and a chocolatier?' said Dad with a thoughtful expression.

'A what?' replied Hero, pleased that his old dad might be back.

'Philanthropist. A person who uses their wealth to help other people less fortunate than themselves.'

'Like Robin Hood?' suggested Hero.

'Hmmm … I wouldn't use that analogy,' said Dad. 'Ramsbottom gave his workers homes to live in with a garden and a pear tree.'

'And the chocolate?' asked Hero, curious.

'It was delicious; I used to love Ramsbottom's Rambo Bars.'

'I mean, did the workers get free chocolate?'

Dad laughed. For a moment, Hero caught a glimpse of his old dad, before he lost himself in knowledge.

'I bet they had their fair share,' he grinned.

After passing the bend of the river, Hero noticed that the factory was no longer straight ahead. It was now on the opposite side of the riverbank.

'We've got to cross,' said Hero, staring down at the foaming water.

Dad forced his mouth into a frown. 'I don't fancy

going in there again. I think my freshwater swimming days are well and truly over.'

Hero continued to walk, thinking of how they could get to the other side.

'**My flip-flops!**' yelled Dad, pointing to a reed bed. 'There's one there, and the other one is just near that rock.'

Hero carefully climbed down the narrow bank and retrieved the flip-flops. Dad grinned, content at being reunited with his mud-covered Union flag footwear. But Hero had a problem to solve. He scanned the area for inspiration.

'**That can help us!**' he said, pointing to a tall, leafless tree.

'How?'

'**Look!**'

A dirty grey rope was wrapped like a vine round one of its thick branches.

Dad scrunched up his eyes. 'A rope swing?'

'We can use it to get to the other side of the river,' said Hero.

Hero climbed up the tree and unravelled the rope, which fell down and hung straight in the air. He pulled on it to make sure the knot was tight.

Dad eyed the twine. 'We'll not get across with that.'

Hero glanced down at Dad, his lips squeezed together. Without having to think, two words came to the surface of his consciousness like bubbles.

'Tarzan physics!'

Dad raised an inquisitive eyebrow.

'Don't you remember?' said Hero. 'You told Mr Roxburgh about it at parents' evening. He had to stop you as people were complaining you were taking too long.'

'Tarzan physics … yes … that's right. It's coming back now.'

Dad's eyes lit up like blue gemstones as he applied his intellect to what had become a problem of physics.

'How was Tarzan able to swing across the jungle on vines?' he asked.

'Because he knew the precise moment he should let go of the rope!' chirped Hero.

'Correct! So, when do we let go of the rope?' asked Dad.

Hero squeezed his eyebrows together, forcing his little grey cells to retrieve the information. He tried his best to ignore Dad when he was in Download Knowledge Mode by nodding and saying 'Yes', 'Interesting', 'Cool'. But now he had to remember.

'I've got it!' blurted Hero. 'To maximise flight distance, Tarzan's angle of release should always be less than forty-five degrees!'

'Well done! You are an *aide-memoire*,' said Dad excitedly. 'I recall ... the horizontal velocity is converted to vertical speed, which sends you upwards in a parabolic trajectory.'

'What?' said Hero, looking puzzled.

'We let go of the rope at the lowest point, near the river.' Dad smiled.

'Oh, I see ... let's do it.'

'Though there's no simple rule,' said Dad with a pensive frown. 'It depends on several factors, such as the length of the rope, its distance from the ground and its angle at the start of the swing and at the time of release.'

'Are we going to do it or not?'

'Of course,' said Dad, swiping the air with his hand. 'We have to prove this hypothesis!'

A few moments later, Hero stood between the two largest branches of the sun-baked tree.

'Are you sure you don't want to go first?' he said, his breath quickening.

'I need to tell you what I can remember,' said Dad. 'Now, you've got to keep your body straight, hang like a pendulum. Then, just before the lowest point, let go of the rope. The velocity should get you to the other side.

'Don't be scared,' said Dad, his voice soft and encouraging.

Hero gripped the rope. It felt wiry and itchy.

'Come on. You can do it!'

Hero narrowed his eyes and stared down at the gurgling river, his heart beating fast and his hands clammy. There was no other way. They couldn't waste any more time. They had to cross. Gran was in danger.

He took a deep breath and leaped into the air.

'Ahhhhhhhhhhh!'

'NOW!' yelled Dad.

Hero let go of the rope, swinging upwards away from the river and towards the bank. He looked down – the water was getting closer, hissing and snarling.

THUD!

'Eureka! You've done it,' yelled Dad.

Hero smiled at Dad from the opposite side of the river as he threw the rope back to him.

'My turn now,' yelled Dad, sticking his flip-flops in each side of his chamois-leather loincloth.

He climbed the tree, took the rope between his hands and without hesitation, jumped.

'GERONIMOoooooo!'

Dad swung through the air in his homemade loincloth like a middle-aged man with an underwear crisis.

He let go of the rope, landing on the other side of the river, where he slid down the bank.

He stretched his arms out, searching for something to grip.

'Come on, Dad!' said Hero, grabbing Dad's arm to help him up the slope. 'You nearly made it.'

Dad released a puff of air.

'I was a millisecond too late,' he said, 'but Tarzan physics didn't let us down.'

'Yeah, we did it,' said Hero.

'Indubitably! But the next challenge is to get into there,' said Dad, pointing behind Hero.

Hero turned to find a metal fence encircling the old chocolate factory.

Beyond the Obvious

'We can't climb over that fence; we'll be cut to pieces,' said Hero, staring up at the glistening barbed wire.

'Do not hide from that which you fear,' Dad replied in a knowledgeable tone.

'What?' said Hero. 'That's something Terra Firma would say.'

'Terra who?' asked Dad, looking bewildered.

'Terra Firma – that's ... that was your name.'

'Hmm ... well, this Terra Firma ... or should I say, me ... is right. Barbed wire is symbolic of an oppressive society,' said Dad. 'Although it is possible to surmount it with a carpet.'

'Well, there's not going to be one around here,' said Hero, doubting whether Dad had recovered.

'That is a logical conclusion.'

'Come on, let's see if we can find a way in,' said Hero.

They trudged along the perimeter of the site until they turned onto a small road at the front of the disused factory. A red-brick wall with washed-out wooden panels replaced the meshed fence, and a tall, rusting, yellowish-brown gate protected the entrance.

Hero gazed up and grinned at an iron arch that used to spell the name of the owner. The letters 'R', 'A', 'M' and 'S' had been removed.

The sign now read:

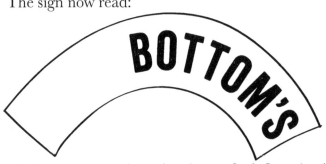

'We've got to get into the site to find Gran,' said Hero.

'I guess that will need thinking beyond the obvious!' replied Dad.

Hero made a puzzled face. 'What do you mean?'

Dad paused and touched his head. 'I don't know. Oh … this synapse lapse is annoying.'

'Wait! What did you used to say?' said Hero, concentrating hard. 'To meet new challenges … we must use solutions … outside the boundaries of ordinary thinking.'

'Absolutely! And all the time I assumed you never listened to a word I said. I was wrong!' said Dad. 'Now let's see what we can do with these panels.'

Hero pressed the first wooden panel inset in the red-brick wall. It remained rigid.

'When it comes to security, we expect intruders will try to enter from the back and side,' said Dad with a glint of wisdom in his eyes.

Hero pushed the other panels, but they stayed in place – except for the last one, which creaked.

'We rarely think intruders have the audacity to use the front door.'

With both hands, Hero pressed hard on the wooden panel. It wobbled. He did it again until the bottom of the panel came away from the wall.

'Cool! We can enter here.'

'Well done, Hero,' beamed Dad.

Hero and Dad squeezed through the loose panel in the wall and crouched in the dry overgrowth that once was the manicured lawns of the old chocolate factory. Rough fragments of glass, stone and concrete were scattered on the ground, where former buildings once stood. The grey corrugated-metal building they had seen from the river towered over two rectangular, mottled, red-brick constructions.

'That's the white van Mr Bugwell said they took Gran away in,' said Hero, peering through weeds.

The van, three cars and two lorries were left like abandoned toys on the gravel path.

'We need to see if Gran is in those buildings over there.'

'Affirmative,' said Dad. 'There may be evidence to prove Mr Bugwell's hypothesis.'

They both left the safety of the undergrowth and scuttled to the side of the corrugated-metal building.

The sound of machinery **clinking and clanking** echoed inside.

'I've got to get up there and find out what's making that noise,' said Hero, pointing to an out-of-reach window.

Hero climbed on Dad's shoulders and was lifted up to the window. He licked his finger and rubbed the grime-covered glass to make a spyhole.

Inside, spotlights lit a cavernous space. In the middle

there was a tall metal tube surrounded by a steel frame, staircase and container, which looked like a control room. There was a handful of overalled workers, with one man sitting at a desk in the far corner of the building, staring at a computer screen.

'What are they doing?' said Dad, holding onto Hero's legs.

'NO WAY! There's a pole in the ground. I think they're **fracking**!'

'Hero … you need to come down,' said Dad in a warning voice.

'Wait! I have to see what they're up to,' said Hero.

'NO! You must come down,' said Dad, gripping tightly to Hero's legs. **'Now!'**

'Why?' said Hero.

He glanced down to see a large coal-black dog at the corner of the building. The beast snarled, revealing sharp white teeth coated in shimmering saliva.

Ethology

Hero jumped down and stuck beside Dad like a limpet to a rock.

'HrrrrrWrrrwrrr.'

The dog gave a low, deep-throat growl. Its face filled with indignation, as if Hero and Dad had just gate-crashed a party.

It barked and moved towards them.

Hero blinked and swallowed hard. His stomach clenched, making him feel sick.

'How are we going to get out of this?' he said through gritted teeth.

'I read a most interesting entry in Cuthbert's encyclopaedia on ethology,' said Dad, holding Hero by the arm. 'I'm sure he mentioned what to do in such situations.'

'Ethology?' quizzed Hero, staring at Dad and then back at the beast.

'The scientific study of animal behaviour!'

'He's coming **CIoooooooooser**,' said Hero, grimacing with fear.

'Yawn, and lick your lips,' said Dad.

'What?' asked Hero, bemused at the suggestion.

'**Aaaaawaaaawh,**' said Dad, opening his mouth widely. '**Mchht, mchht, mchht.**'

Hero gave a desperate yawn.

'**Aaaaawaaaawh. Mchht, mchht, mchht.**'

The dog stopped and looked on, mystified by their actions.

'It's calming behaviour, to signal passivity,' said Dad, edging backwards, pulling Hero with him.

'Protect your vulnerable bits!'

'**Dad! Stop it!**' said Hero, clenching his fists.

'I was merely saying the primary target of a canine

is your throat and groin,' squeaked Dad.

The animal moved forward and barked again.

'NO!' said Hero, in a low, firm voice.

The dog snarled in protest.

'Go away!'

It pricked up its ears and turned its head.

'Stalin! Come!' said a heavily accented voice in the distance.

Stalin eyed Hero and Dad and then glared back.

'Stalin! Food!'

The clanging, tinny sound of a dish was all that the beast needed to decide that food was more attractive than intruders.

It ran off.

'Stalin! Where've you been, boy?' said the voice.

'Phew! That was close,' said Hero, wiping his brow with his hand.

'It did cause a stiffening of the sinews and a summoning up of the blood,' said Dad, relieved. 'Well done!'

'Quick, let's see if Gran is over there,' said Hero, eager to take cover.

They both ran back into the undergrowth and continued towards a red-brick rectangular building.

'This looks like the old foreman's office and store,' said Dad, crouching at the side of the building.

Hero peered over a wooden windowsill with grey flaking paint. The windows were blacked out, but one had a piece of glass missing in the corner, allowing him to glimpse inside.

An incandescent lightbulb hung from the ceiling, working hard in the dripping darkness. The shadows of rusting, doorless cabinets lingered alongside the walls.

'It's Gran!' whispered Hero, relieved to see her.

Gran was sitting in a wooden chair in a darkened corner with a rope wrapped around her body.

'They've got her tied up!'

'Wait! Is there anyone else in there? We need to undertake a full risk assessment,' said Dad.

Hero squinted through the broken pane.

A door opened, and a lanky, overalled man walked in carrying a silver tray with a tall glass decorated with a pink straw, a sunrise-yellow umbrella and a slice of orange.

'Now, that doesn't look too bad,' Hero heard Gran say.

The lanky henchmen presented the drink to Gran, positioning a straw between her lips.

She took a slurp.

'Mmmm …' she said. 'You're nearly there, but it needs a bit more sugar and a little less lemon.'

The overalled man dropped his head in disappointment.

'Don't be disheartened, dear. The temple of Hatshepsut wasn't built in a day. You've all the ingredients; you've just got to get the quantities right. You know, when I used to work in the cocktail bar many moons ago …'

Gran babbled away about her job with the famous bartender Cocktail Colin.

'I'll check out the front of the building,' whispered Hero, scuttling off.

'But, Hero …' said Dad.

A few minutes later, Hero returned.

'Is he still there?' Hero said.

'He certainly is.' Dad nodded wearily. 'If she carries on like this, we may have to rescue *him*.'

'I've got a plan,' declared Hero, explaining what he wanted to do.

'Hmm … it's risky, but there's no other option,' whispered Dad. 'Go for it, but be careful.'

After some time, the lanky henchman yawned, made some excuse and left the room.

Hero hurried to the front of the building and peeked round the corner. Balancing a silver tray in one hand, the henchman was attempting to close a padlock on the door.

Hero got in position, pretending he was in the football stadium taking a penalty in the World Cup. He ran towards an empty tin can and whacked it into the air. The tin sped across the site, hitting the corrugated-metal construction.

The lanky henchman nearly dropped the tray at the distraction. The dog barked in the distance. Composing himself, he went to investigate.

At that point, Dad scurried from the other side of the building to the door, turned the hook on the padlock to make it appear to be locked and returned to the corner.

The henchman came back and stared at the door, scratching his blond hair. On seeing that the padlock was apparently locked, he carried on with his tray to the corrugated-metal building.

Hero waited a few minutes until he was sure the coast was clear and hurried to the door, where he met Dad.

'Well done. You've got the gist of thinking beyond the obvious,' said Dad.

Hero smiled; his plan had worked. He unhooked the padlock.

'Come on, Dad. Let's get Gran out of here before they find us.'

'I am afraid you're too late,' said a familiar voice.

Hero turned to discover a stocky man with a red goatee beard, beaming a menacing grin.

'Good boy, Stalin,' said Dimitri, patting the dog on his head.

Parry and Riposte

'**Ouch!** You're hurting me,' said Hero, struggling to set himself free.

A stocky, hairy henchman wearing a green overall pushed Hero down and tied him to the wooden chair with a thick rope.

'Let me go!' he demanded.

'I would appreciate it if you were more careful with my son,' protested Dad.

'You are the famous earth warrior?' said the hairy henchman in his strong accent. 'Not so brave now, are ya, eh?' He shoved Dad forward.

'Wait till Mr Vump sees him,' laughed the other henchman, who was equally as large but hairless. 'He'll be disappointed. The dog has more meat on him than this bone.'

'Hero, is that you?' said a voice from the blackness.

'Gran!' yelled Hero.

'Eddie, are you there too?' enquired Gran.

'Yes, it is me.'

'Why aren't you protecting the Rec?'

'Gran! We came to rescue you,' said Hero eagerly. 'Dad's got his memory back.'

'Hero has told me about this unfortunate state of affairs,' said Dad.

'I suppose the fight for the Rec is over now you're back,' said Gran. 'I was looking forward to a good scrap.'

'Mother! You should know better at your age.'

'You shouldn't have come. I can manage the situation,' said Gran, her shadow nodding in the corner.

'But you're tied up like a donkey,' said Hero, tugging at his rope.

'This is nothing compared to the time Ethel and I were taken captive by the Mexican crime lord,' said Gran. 'It was the infamous Heriberto Juan Esparragozolo. Anyway, we thought we were guacamole—'

'I'm sorry to interrupt your family reunion,' snorted the hairy henchman, 'but we have work to do.'

He thrust Dad in the direction of the chair. Dad  to the floor.

A mobile rang. The hairless henchman pulled a phone out from his pocket and spoke in a language Hero didn't understand.

'I leave you in the capable hands of my colleague,' he said with a sarcastic grin.

He talked a bit more on his mobile before leaving the room.

'Get up, you dog,' said the hairy henchman.

Dad rose to his feet.

The henchmen seized Dad's arm but Dad resisted and pulled away. He grabbed Dad from behind, trying to get him in a neck lock.

Before Hero knew it, the hairy henchman was flying over Dad's head.

yelled Hero, incredulous.

'Where …? How …?' said the henchman, lost for words. He lay on the floor rubbing his head, stunned that a skinny weakling could ever lift a brawny man like him, never mind throw him in the air.

At the realisation of his humiliating defeat, the hairy henchman struggled to his feet and charged towards Dad like a raging bull.

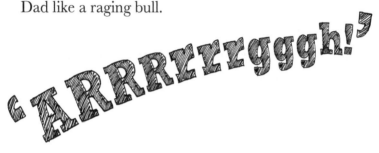

'ARRRrrgggh!'

Dad leaped out of his path and fixed his arms into a martial arts position.

'It's the Karate Kid!' yelled Gran.

The henchman charged again, but Dad, being nimble on his feet, jumped out of the way.

'How are you able to do that?' said Hero, finding words.

'Cuthbert's encyclopaedia. I read a whole entry on the essentials of self-defence,' said Dad, smiling in the dull light.

The hairy henchman's face was now as red as a beef tomato. He grabbed a long piece of scrap metal from the corner and swiped at the air as if it were a lightsabre.

He chased Dad around the room, but Dad was too fast.

While the henchman was gasping for breath, Dad grabbed another metal strip.

'I'm also fully versed in Diego de Valera's *Treatise on Arms*!' he declared.

'What?' said Hero, overwhelmed by all the action.

Dad took up a fencing position and attacked the henchman with his blade, but the henchmen blocked it.

'He's bloomin' Errol Flynn now!' said Gran.

'Apparently, it's one of the oldest surviving manuals on western fencing,' said Dad as he went in for another attack.

'Who? What?' marvelled Hero.

'He was an old Hollywood movie star,' said Gran.

Hero shook his head, confused.

Meanwhile, Dad seemed to enjoy the impromptu fencing so much he failed to notice the hairless henchman appear from the shadows.

'Dad!' shouted Hero, trying to catch his attention.

But Dad continued to parry and riposte around the room, taking the hairy henchman on a merry dance. That was until the hairless henchman stepped into the light, pointing a black revolver at Dad. Dad froze and raised his arms above his head.

The hairy henchman hit Dad on the head with a steel bucket, causing Dad to collapse into a heap on the floor.

36

Mr Vump

Sometime

later the door opened,

and a shaft of light flashed

across the darkened room.

Footsteps echoed in the hollow building.

'Oh no ...' muttered Hero. 'This doesn't feel good.'

A shadowy outline of a small man with silver hair tied back in a ponytail appeared, wearing a black suit and brown snakeskin boots with Cuban heels. He was followed by Dimitri.

'So this is the famous earth warrior?' said Barnabas Vump in a gravelly voice.

'Yes, sir,' replied Dimitri.

Dad was still unconscious on the floor.

'What a great disappointment. I imagined a brave and strong warrior, not some wimp,' said Vump with an evil laugh.

He turned to Gran and scowled.

'And you are the rebellious protestor that ruined my operation in Nigeria,' he sneered.

'And you are the ruthless energy tycoon who doesn't care for anything but profit!' returned Gran defiantly.

'Let us go!' yelled Hero, sounding more confident than he felt. 'If we are not back soon, my friends will call the police.'

Vump snorted, waving away the words before glaring at Dad. 'Wake him!'

The hairless henchman threw a bucket of water over Dad.

Dad groaned and came to life.

'Does the brave warrior have nothing to say?' said Vump with a sarcastic tone. 'I am in charge now. I am the leader, the chief, your master!'

'You can do what you want with me, but let my son and his gran go,' said Dad weakly, his head down.

'No! Dad,' yelled Hero, his seat wobbling in protest.

'Hah! You have all caused me much distress and cost me a great deal of money,' said Vump. His heels clicked and clacked as he walked up and down.

'First in Nigeria and now in Leaford,' he said. 'Paying off Onions and the state governor was not cheap.'

'You mean you bribed Onions to buy the Rec?' exclaimed Hero.

'SHOCKING!' shouted Gran. 'I knew that state governor was in cahoots with you, and that Leaford Council wouldn't have agreed. I used to be a good friend of the Lord Mayor, you know. Alfred and I—'

'ENOUGH!' yelled Vump, stomping his Cuban heels on the concrete floor.

'Well, I'm sorry for any inconvenience caused,' said Dad, trying to calm Vump down.

'You don't have to apologise to him,' said Hero sharply.

Vump grinned in the faint light as the henchmen lifted Dad from the floor and tied him in the chair.

'Hah! You and your protestors are all pathetic. You will never stop my energy revolution.'

'You took the only green space where we can play football,' said Hero. 'Why are you doing all this?'

'Why?' screeched Vump, his small body exploding in hand gestures. 'I tell you why. Because I spent my childhood imprisoned in an orphanage listening to environmental claptrap from people like you. We had nothing new. Only recycled, worn-out clothes and broken toys. They refused to use coal and gas because they wanted to save the planet. We had to put up with unreliable solar power and foul-smelling bio-waste.'

'Sounds great,' said Dad.

'Great? Was it not enough that we were denied the love of parents? But also to be deprived of the glow of a blazing fire in the cold, dark winters, and toys that worked?'

Hero blinked. 'What's all this got to do with us?'

'On those freezing nights when I couldn't feel my

hands and toes, I dreamed that one day everyone would have all the energy and warmth they needed and green fanatics like you would be silenced forever,' said Vump. He gave out a manic laugh. 'They thought my ideas were strange. They thought I was too small to achieve anything. I showed them all!'

'Let us go!'

yelled Hero, realising that Vump was more doolally than his Great Uncle Dave. 'You can't keep us here.'

'I can do what I want with you,' snapped Vump. He flashed a wicked grin.

'What are you going to do with us?'

Vump crossed his arms and purred. 'You need to be eliminated from the equation.'

Hero's heart missed a beat.

'Once the earth warrior has gone, these protestors will soon get bored.'

'Don't worry, Hero,' said Dad. 'I can see that Mr Vump is not a megalomaniac; he won't extinguish a young life. I'm sure he wants all kids to enjoy a warm fire.'

Vump grinned as if he had just sucked on a lemon.

'You are a perceptive man.'

'What are you going to do with us?' repeated Hero worriedly.

'I am sending you far away from here, where you can no longer interfere in my business.'

Hero tugged at his wrist; his skin stung as he squeezed it through the knotted rope.

'Where?'

'Tomorrow my ship leaves for Easter Island to start my new fracking operation. You'll be among its cargo and will be put to work when we arrive. Consider it an act of charity.'

'Easter Island? Where's that?' said Hero.

'I know … wait a moment … it's coming …' said Dad, straining his forehead. 'Yes, I've got it! The south-easternmost point of the Polynesian Triangle in the Pacific Ocean.'

'Is that the place with all those stone heads?' Gran asked from the dark corner.

'It is. If I recall correctly, the Rapa Nui people created eight hundred and eighty-seven stone monuments called Moai.'

'It will be the first trip without Ethel,' said Gran, her eyes welling up. 'I'll miss the old gal, but at least she's found love in the desert.'

'ARRRrrrgggh!'

cried Hero, his face smarting with anger. 'What are you talking about? They're kidnapping us. We'll be prisoners. We're not going on a holiday.'

'ENOUGH!' yelled Vump, stomping his foot again. 'You'll be removed from this place tomorrow once and for all. My plans to frack will go ahead without you and your silly protestors.'

Vump swivelled on his heels and crossed the room.

Hero tugged hard at the rope, setting one hand free. He pulled the other hand through the twine, grating his skin.

'Dad,' whispered Hero. 'I will extinguish Edison!'

'Go for it!' smiled Dad. 'I'll follow.'

With that, Hero unleashed himself from the rope, dashed across to the wall and switched off the light, causing the dimly lit room to descend into blackness.

THUD!

'ARRRrrrgggh!! YOU IMBECILES!'

BANG!

WHACK!

'GET THEM!

OUCH!

GET

OFF

ME!'

When the light was switched on again, Hero was cornered by Vump's henchmen.

Dad was on the floor, unconscious.

'NOT AGAIN!' cried Hero

and Gran in unison.

The hairy henchman smiled as he threw another bucket of water over Dad.

Vump gave an evil laugh. 'What a feeble attempt to escape.'

Dad groaned.

'Get up, you dog!' yelled Vump.

Dad staggered to his feet.

He stood tall, towering over Vump.

'There are two types of dog,' Dad said pensively. 'One is brave. The other is a coward. A brave dog dies but once, but a coward dog dies many times.'

'And what type of dog are you?' grinned Vump.

Dad puffed out his chest and raised his chin in the air. 'I am Terra Firma, chief of the earth warriors. I die only once.'

'He's back!' yelled Hero.

'I wish he'd decide whether he's coming or going,' said Gran.

Vump stared at Dad with a blank expression on his face and stepped backwards.

'DIMITRI! Deal with them!'

he ordered.

Dimitri and the henchmen swiftly tied Hero and Dad back to the chairs.

'Let us go!' protested Hero.

Dad didn't put up a fight but remained quiet in thought.

'We will have no more trouble from them now, sir,' said the hairy henchman.

Suddenly, the lanky overalled man burst through the door. 'Sir, we've had a malfunction. I suggest we evacuate the site immediately.'

Vump glowered angrily.

'We misjudged the pressure of the waste-water injection,' added the lanky henchman. 'It was too high. We think we've set off a wave of seismic activity.'

'You imbecile!'

growled Vump, spitting out the words in disgust. 'If they find out what we have been doing, we will lose our licence.'

'What are they talking about?' asked Gran.

'I *told* him to concentrate on his cocktail making.'

'They've already been doing fracking,' said Hero.

'You mean drilling for gas, here too?'

'Yeah!'

'Disgraceful! Cecil Ramsbottom would be turning in his grave,' said Gran, nodding in the gloom.

Without warning, the building trembled. It was as if it had woken up in a bad temper after a century of sleep. It spat out dust in protest, grinding its girders and stretching its bricks of muscle.

The row of rusting, doorless cabinets clinked and clanked as they chattered away.

'Let us go!' cried Hero, his heart racing.

The building shuddered again, and dust came raining down like a giant's dandruff.

'What shall we do with them, sir?' Dimitri asked.

Vump paused and rubbed his chin. He then smirked with a glint of madness in his eye.

'Hah!' he said, laughing unconvincingly.

'The building could collapse,' said Hero, swallowing hard.

'How very convenient.' Vump hurried past the rusty cabinets towards the door. But before he could reach it, the ground entered a fit of convulsions, jerking and jolting in all directions. Pieces of timber, broken tiles and bricks tumbled down, and cabinets collapsed to the floor.

'Nooooooooooooo!'

cried Hero.

Clever Levers

Rays of sunshine shone through the remains of the roof, lighting up the room that had become a dump of dirt and debris.

Hero gasped for air as decades of dust fogged the place. He coughed to clear his throat and rid his mouth of the gritty sawdust taste.

'Hero! Where are you?' wheezed Gran.

Hero tugged hard at his binding, releasing himself. He spat and rubbed his eyes on the back of his hands, then rushed over to the remains of the corner. Gran was on the floor, tied to a wooden chair, which had cracked in two.

'Are you all right?' he asked, setting her free.

Gran coughed several times, her face grimed like a coal miner's.

'I feel awful,' she said. 'The last time I was this bad was after Raj's Diwali party. He was such a lovely man. He knew how—'

'Where's Dad?' Hero surveyed the room, trying to recognise the layout. Some of the rusting, doorless cabinets that stood alongside the wall were now on the floor. A large cabinet had fallen in the exact place where Dad had been sitting in the corner.

'**NOooooooooo!**' Hero yelled.

A shot of adrenalin burned through his veins. He scurried over the rubble.

'**Dad! Dad!**'

He tried to lift the cabinet, but it wouldn't budge.

'**Dad!**' he yelled again, letting a tear escape onto his cheek.

He banged his fist on the metal in frustration. The sound echoed like a steel drum.

'Steady on!' said a voice.

Hero raised his eyebrows in surprise.

He thumped again.

'Is that you, Dad … errr … Terra Firma?'

'Yes, it's me, but please don't knock so loudly,' said

Dad. 'I now know what it is to be a sardine in a tin.'

Hero slipped his fingers under the rusty edge of the cabinet. He gripped it tightly and, using all his strength, he tried to raise it from the ground.

'I can't lift it, Dad. It's too heavy.'

'Hmm ... another challenge of the day,' reverberated Dad.

'I must get help, but it might take time,' said Hero.

'Oh ... this synapse lapse is so debilitating in a crisis,' complained Dad.

Hero held his breath, thinking what to do – then a word sprang into his head like a jack jumping out of a box.

'See-saw!' blurted Hero. 'We can try a see-saw!'

'Yes! Let's try leverage,' said Dad, his voice echoing.

'What are you talking about?' said Gran, looking on astonished.

'The see-saw is a lever; it can help lift the cabinet,' said Hero.

'Hmm ...' said Gran, scanning the chaos.

'We need to use a piece of wood,' said Hero, trying to lift a beam that had fallen from the ceiling. 'Urggh ... it's too much.'

Gran came over and together they tried again.

'It's as heavy as a whale,' gasped Gran.

'What about that over there?' said Hero, crawling across the rubble. They struggled to pick up a plank of wood but managed to move it to the cabinet by determinedly pushing and pulling at it.

'Now what?' said Gran.

'Fulcrum! Don't forget you need a pivot point for the lever,' resonated Dad from under his metal enclosure.

Hero assembled some broken bricks and moved the wood into position.

'Are you ready, Dad?' said Hero. 'I hope it works.'

The cabinet rumbled and banged. 'Go ahead!'

'Come on, Gran. Sit on the wood, and let's try to lift up the cabinet. I'll help Dad out.'

Hero placed the edge of the plank under the lip of the cabinet.

Gran sat down on the wooden plank with all the determination of a sulking rhinoceros. As she did so, the other end of the plank rose in the air, pushing the rusting box upwards, creating a small gap between the cabinet and floor.

'It's not wide enough,' said Hero, disappointed.

'You sit with Gran,' shouted Dad.

'You won't be able to get out.'

'Just do it!'

Hero sat next to Gran on the edge of the wood. The extra weight widened the gap between the floor and the cabinet.

'What now?' said Hero.

Before Dad could respond, two hands appeared and pushed the cabinet upwards, setting himself free.

"Voila!" exclaimed a grey and dusty Dad.

The cabinet fell to the floor.

'How did you untie yourself?'

'I've read about the famous illusionist Houdini and have learned a few of his tricks,' declared Dad.

Suddenly, another rusty cabinet vibrated.

'Where's Vump?' asked Hero.

'The last time I saw them, they were running off,' said Gran.

Hero moved closer to the fallen cabinet.

'**Help! Help!** Let me out,' said a voice. 'I hate confined spaces – please, please. I beg you.'

'Let them stay there,' snorted Hero.

'It would be inhumane to allow them to perish,' said Dad with a frown.

Hero gave a disappointed sigh. 'I guess you're right.'

He picked up the wood they had just used for the see-saw.

'Come on, Dad, let's do it again.'

They balanced the plank for a second time on a pile of bricks, placing one end under the lip of the cabinet.

'What if they run off?' asked Hero.

'We should call the police. They need locking up,' added Gran.

'What a cynical lot you are,' said Dad. 'Have faith in human nature. They will not escape in these conditions.'

Hero flashed an unconvinced glance at Gran.

'Sit down, then!'

Gran and Hero sat down on the end of the plank, and the cabinet rose from the floor. Dad helped to lift it up, allowing Vump and Dimitri to crawl out from beneath like cockroaches.

Vump panted, taking in air.

'I'm very sorry, sir,' said Dimitri, brushing the dust off Vump's shoulders. 'The others have abandoned us.'

'I employ imbeciles,' spat Vump.

'We must leave, sir. This building is not safe,' said Dimitri.

Vump smirked.

Before Hero had time to think, Vump and Dimitri darted for the door that now hung off its hinges.

'Come on, chaps, can we be sensible about this?' called out Dad.

'Stop them, Eddie!'

shrieked Gran, throwing her arms into the air.

Hero gave a desperate whimper before rushing after them, out of the building and into the intense sunlight.

'Wait for me! We can do this with peaceful negotiation,' said Dad, running after him, followed by Gran.

Without warning, the ground went into a frenzy of **spasms**. More bricks crashed to the floor as dirty grey dust blanketed the air. Hero glanced back over his shoulder as the building

CRUMBLED AWAY, PLUMMETING DOWNWARDS INTO ITSELF.

The Harley Gals

A cloud of dust leaped up into the air as the remains of the building vanished from sight into the ground.

'**DAD!**' howled Hero, his voice resonating throughout his bones.

As the fine dirt dispersed, Hero could make out the shapes of Dad and Gran.

Dad coughed heavily. 'I truly thought that was my demise,' he croaked.

With his eyes gleaming with relief, Dad looked at Hero. 'Come here, let's have a hug sandwich.'

With that, he swept Hero up into a hug and grabbed Gran by surprise, squeezing Hero between them. A warm sensation spread through Hero like hot chocolate on a cold winter's day.

With his darkened face and dust-encrusted hair, Dad flashed a white smile.

'I thought you'd forgotten about hug sandwiches,' said Hero.

'No, I'd never forget it. I … well … it wasn't the same without your mum.'

Hero surrendered a smile that was tugging at the side of his mouth.

'Some suggest that humans require eight hugs a day to stay happy. I am not sure of the scientific validity of such a statement, but what I know is that I've been rather neglectful in that department.'

'I'm glad you've come to your senses,' said Gran. 'Now, let's get out of here before anything else happens.'

'You're right. That tremor was much stronger than before. There may be an aftershock!' said Dad.

They all hurried towards the main entrance of the old chocolate factory, where the iron gates were wide open.

'I bet Vump has got away,' said Hero, shielding his eyes from the sunlight.

'I would've left them under that cabinet,' said Gran.

'That's cruel,' protested Dad. 'I'm sure they'll get their comeuppance.'

'Over there!' yelled Hero, pointing down the road.

Vump and Dimitri were sitting inside a dusty black four-by-four surrounded by purple-leather-clad women on Harley-Davidson motorbikes.

'My gals have done it!' trumpeted Gran like an elephant.

Hero, Dad and Gran advanced towards the pack of roaring motorbikes.

'Rosangela!' said a bronze-faced lady in a purple helmet. 'How are you, pet?'

'Ethel! What are you doing here?' said Gran with an unexpected joy.

Hero beamed a smile at seeing Gran's old friend and his honorary Auntie Ethel.

'I heard all about your Eddie on the radio in the Sudan,' said Ethel with a big grin, revealing the gap between her teeth. 'I had to come and see for myself. This smart young gal contacted Doreen and told us you were in danger.'

A girl on the back of the motorbike removed her helmet.

'Surprise!' exclaimed Mitzy.

'What ...? How ...?' stuttered Hero, not quite recognising Mitzy without her glasses.

Mitzy smiled and swept away the fringe from her eyes. She took her glasses from her pocket and put them on.

'We went to the tent to find you,' she said.

'Yeah, I saw you waving me off on the riverbank,' said Hero.

'We were trying to stop you, stupid!'

Hero gave a nervous grin and glanced at his feet.

'Bugwell said you'd gone to the old chocolate factory. I knew you'd need help to rescue your gran – that's if you survived the river. I Googled the Harley Gals and got the phone number of Doreen, the secretary, and explained about your gran being in danger. She told Ethel, and here we are!'

'She's a smart gal, this one,' said Ethel. 'A true Harley Gal in the making! We must give her an honorary membership. We could do with her techno skills to revamp our website.'

Mitzy raised her chin, puffed out her chest and grinned.

'Does that mean you're staying?' asked Hero.

Ethel nodded enthusiastically.

'What about your husband, the chief?' asked Gran.

'I've left him. I couldn't be bothered with all that sand,' declared Ethel. 'He won't miss me; he's got five other wives to keep him company. Anyway, I would much rather be out on the road with the Gals.'

At that moment, sirens squealed in the distance.

Back on Track

'Your grandfather would have been so proud to have a disorder named after the family,' said Gran, placing a jug on the kitchen table.

It was a week later. Hero and Partha were studying the front page of the *Leaford Bugle* and drinking Gran's ice-cold lemonade.

'What's it called again?' she said.

'The consultant we saw named it Imaginatio Troughominis,' replied Hero.

'To think our Eddie is the only person in the world to have had it,' said Gran, her eyes twinkling with pride. 'Though I'm glad your father is back on track and Heatwave Blistering Bertha has moved on,' she said, putting down a plate of home-made biscuits.

Partha grabbed one and examined it before nibbling at the edges.

'My Tunisian fig and prune delights – guaranteed to keep you regular!' said Gran.

Partha made a face of disgust before realising they didn't taste as bad as they sounded. 'What are you going to do if he turns warrior again?' he said.

'It's unlikely,' said Hero, sipping his lemonade. 'But they just don't know.'

'This whole warrior episode was worse than the time Ethel and I got stuck in the Bangweulu swamps,' said Gran. 'We'd taken the wrong turn at the antelope-skull crossroads. I told her—'

'How did your dad get his memory back, anyway?' asked Partha, turning to Hero as he dabbed up the biscuit crumbs with his finger.

'It could have been the shock of falling in the river. The other theory is that when Dad was in his imaginatio state, he wanted to become a chief and have a tribe. The consultant said that as soon as Dad realised he had achieved his goal, a chemical reaction occurred in his brain, allowing him to return to his normal self. We'll never be sure.'

Partha squeezed his lips together before starting on another biscuit.

At that moment, Mitzy breezed through the kitchen door.

'Sorry I'm late,' she said. 'Dad got confused with the on-and-off button on the remote control and caused a power surge. Leia started speaking gobbledegook, the air conditioning froze the house, the postman couldn't get up the path. We had to reset everything – **Mum's furious**!'

'Technology! Where will it all end?' sighed Gran. 'But never mind, dear, help yourself to a drink and a biscuit.'

Mitzy sat down and poured a glass of lemonade.

'They've postponed the plans for fracking,' reported Hero.

'I read the online edition of the *Bugle* this morning,' replied Mitzy coolly. 'They're going to investigate whether Vump's illegal fracking caused the earthquake.'

'And whether Vump paid off Onions and his cronies to agree to selling off the land,' added Hero, proud that he had told the police about the bribery.

'Miss Flowerdew will be pleased,' chimed in Partha. 'She was so upset when the barricade fell down after the aftershock and damaged her scooter. Walking Bear and Barefoot had to carry her off. I'll miss Terra Firma, but I'm glad we didn't get taken into care. I bet the food would have been awful.'

'Did you see that Mr Bugwell now has a weekly column in the *Bugle*?' said Mitzy with a smug smile.

'No way!' exclaimed Hero.

'It's called "The Word on the Street", and it's about local issues.'

'That's all we need!' said Hero. 'He'll be bugging everyone even more for gossip.'

'And that Slapnatch fellow has left the council. He's moved to Cornwall,' added Mitzy.

'Good riddance to old hamster face!' said Hero.

'All ready now, Hero,' said Dad, entering the kitchen. He stood fully dressed. His face was tanned and fresh, his salt-and-pepper hair neatly parted.

'I've squeezed in my new England flip-flops your gran bought me,' he said. **'Come on!** We've got twenty-eight minutes and thirty seconds to get to the station.'

Hero stood up and grinned so much his cheeks ached.

'I told you I had everything under control,' said Dad, ruffling Hero's hair.

Hero giggled to himself. He couldn't believe Dad had got the World Cup tickets months ago and wanted to keep it a surprise. He had screwed up the *Goal!*

magazine article not because he wasn't interested but because he no longer needed it.

'I'm going to see Waggie play in the World Cup!' said Hero, proud as a peacock in a plumage parade.

'The 15.00 train for Brussels will depart from platform four,' reverberated a voice throughout the station. A crowd of football supporters clad in red, white and blue and waving England flags hurried past the window.

'We should leave in four minutes and twenty-five seconds,' said Dad, staring at his watch.

He stood up and lifted down a small blue suitcase from a shelf above Hero's head and placed it on the seat next to him. He opened it and took out a brown-leather folder the size of a notebook, then returned the case to the overhead shelf.

'It was so kind of Mitzy to brief me on my new e-reader,' said Dad. 'Now I can take my book collection with me wherever I go. I can carry over a thousand books in this small electronic device!'

Hero nodded.

Dad opened the folder and read. After a few seconds, he stopped and gazed up at Hero.

'Mind you, it is always good to talk,' he said.

Hero gave an awkward grin.

'I do miss chatting to your mum. There's not one day or hour I don't think about her,' said Dad, his voice muffled with emotion. 'Her smile, the way she wore her hair, small silly things really.' He turned to the window. 'It's been hard, Hero. I miss her so much.'

'Me too,' said Hero, his lower lip quivering.

'I know it's been difficult for you. I'm sorry I missed your big moment at Prize Day. But things will change from now on.'

Dad turned to Hero and smiled, his eyes glistening.

'At the top of the list is going to the World Cup. Now come here!' he said, opening his arms.

Hero stretched his arms across the small table to hug Dad. A feeling of cheerfulness washed over him. Dad might be a bookworm with a tendency to bore people daft, but at least he was here; he wasn't a warrior and he was his dad.

'I still can't believe you were convinced that you were an earth warrior,' said Hero, leaning back into his seat.

'The human mind is a mysterious thing. With one hundred billion cells and one hundred trillion synapses, it's not surprising that sometimes things go wrong,' said Dad. 'Were you aware that there are three hundred times more connections in the brain than stars in the Milky Way?'

Hero grinned, not knowing what to say.

'As the neurologist concluded, the probability of it ever happening again is low,' said Dad. 'Although I'm surprised it happened in the first place.'

Hero felt a pang of guilt. He had no choice but to tell Dad he had dislodged the shelves and that it was all his fault.

'Don't be silly!' laughed Dad. 'It's more likely to be down to my poor DIY skills.'

A few minutes later, the doors **beeped** before **SLAMMING CLOSED**.

As the Eurostar set off, Hero pulled out of his backpack a crumpled edition of *Goal!* magazine that claimed to have all you needed to know about the World Cup.

Dad played with the leather case in his hands, turning it around, sliding his finger along the edge.

'Why don't you read your book?' said Hero.

Dad twitched a smile.

'Well, if you don't mind. I'm reading a most intriguing chapter about European pirates,' he said.

Dad opened the leather case and started to read.

Hero gazed at the blur of green, white and blue that passed by the window as the train whizzed along. He noticed his reflection in the glass, and for one moment he was sure he could see the outline of Mum's face, beaming at him.

He smiled, wondering if he had been the change he wanted to see or whether it was just a lucky turn of events. Either way, Terra Firma had helped Dad return to his old self, and, as Gran said, things were now back on track.

'Hero, you'll find this very interesting,' said Dad, studying his e-reader.

'Did you know that the most famous European pirate was—'

SCREEEeeeeeccch!

The train **shuddered** to a halt, throwing Hero and Dad off their seats.

The suitcase on the overhead shelf came

CRASHING DOWN,

hitting Dad's head and knocking him to the ground like a feeble skittle.

'Dad! Dad!' yelled Hero, not believing he could be out cold again.

Hero struggled to lift Dad off the floor, and with some effort he got him back up on the seat.

He checked his pulse and breathing.

'What's happened here?' said a flushed-faced football supporter, poking his head over the seat behind.

'It's my dad. He's been knocked out,' gasped Hero.

'GƦƦƦƦƦƦƦƦƦƦƦƦƦƦƦƦƦƦ,' groaned Dad.

'He must be coming round now,' said the football supporter. 'Don't worry, lad, he'll just have a humungous headache!'

Hero looked at Dad.

Something was different.

He stared hard at Dad's face.

It didn't have that familiar placid look.

It seemed contorted with a curious expression.

It was as if Dad were someone else …

WHAT IS FRACKING?

Fracking is a process used to extract oil and gas from the earth. It involves drilling a hole into the ground, then injecting water, sand and chemicals into rock at a high pressure. This creates cracks in the rock, allowing oil and gas to flow out and be collected.

Fracking allows difficult to reach oil and gas reserves to be used. This is considered important as traditional supplies of oil, coal and gas are decreasing. Supporters of fracking claim it not only creates new jobs, but ensures we have energy in the future.

However, fracking requires lots of water and people worry that the chemicals used could contaminate drinking water and affect health. Gas reserves may be in green spaces that people do not want to change.

Fracking has also been linked to earthquakes as drilling can cause earth tremors. Green groups believe we should reduce our demand for energy and use clean energy sources, such as solar and wind instead, as gas contributes to climate change.

GROWING UP IN A CHANGING CLIMATE

A theme throughout this story has been the **change in the weather**. If you ask your grandparents, parents or older relatives about what the weather was like when they were young, they might say they had milder summers or colder winters or more distinct seasons than we have today.

Sun, rain or snow, the conditions outside affect how we feel and how we live our daily lives. The weather we experience is influenced by changes in the global climate.

The atmosphere is a thin layer of gases around the Earth, like the skin of an apple. Climate is how this atmosphere 'behaves' over a long period. It is the average weather over time and space. But, weather can change from minute to minute, hour to hour or month to month.

One way to remember the difference is that climate is what you expect, such as sunshine on your summer holidays at the beach, while weather is what you get on the day, for example, **THUNDERSTORMS** and **rain**!

Scientists have been monitoring the concentration of gases in the atmosphere and have found some gases have been increasing. The main culprit is **carbon dioxide** (CO_2) which is released when we burn fossil fuels, such as oil, coal and gas. These gases stay in the atmosphere and contribute to the warming of the Earth. They call this the **'greenhouse effect'** because a greenhouse traps the heat from the sun and makes it warm.

The increase in emissions of CO_2 and other greenhouse gases in the atmosphere makes the blanket of gases surrounding the Earth thicker. This thick blanket of gases is trapping more heat and causing **global warming** and our climate to change.

As the planet warms, we can expect extreme weather. This could be more heat waves, droughts, floods and storms.

We are already seeing the consequences of a changing climate. It is therefore vital we reduce the emissions of greenhouse gases.

Most of the energy we consume comes from **BURNING FOSSIL FUELS**. We all produce CO_2 from the goods and services we use. Things we do every day, such as turning on the heating, playing computer games, washing, eating food, travelling by car to school or the shops and flying on holiday, contribute to our personal carbon emissions.

The total amount of CO_2 produced by a country, individual, household or school is known as a **carbon footprint** and is measured in tonnes of CO_2. The size of the carbon footprint varies according to how much energy we use.

If we all tread lightly and lessen our carbon footprint, our impact on the environment will be reduced and we can all contribute to tackling climate change.

If you would like to learn more about climate change and what you can do about it, turn over the page to find a few useful places to start.

BOOK

Climate Change

by HRH The Prince of Wales, Tony Juniper and Emily Shuckburgh.

WEBSITES

EcoFriendlyKids:

www.ecofriendlykids.co.uk

National Geographic Kids:

https://www.natgeokids.com/au/discover/
geography/general-geography/what-is-climate-
change/

Calculate your family's footprint

http://footprint.wwf.org.uk/

JOIN THE
EARTH WARRIORS!

The Earth is our mother, our life-support system, our home. We depend on it for the air we breathe, the water we drink and the food we eat. It provides us with shelter and warmth and all the materials that allow us to live our lives to the full.

We need to take care of it, protect it, and make sure it's in good shape, not only for ourselves but for future generations.

So far, we have not been doing a great job. Human pressure has caused our natural systems to be damaged. We have polluted and plundered the planet, affecting the delicate connections in the web of life.

While we have improved the situation in some areas,

more needs to be done. We can all be earth warriors and take action to protect **MOTHER EARTH**!

While some actions may have to wait until you are older, there are things you can do right now. Why not join the tribe and become an earth warrior?

HERE ARE A FEW IDEAS:

1 SWITCH OFF

Turn off lights and electrical appliances when not in use. This saves money on the electricity bill and reduces your carbon footprint.

2 CLEAN YOUR PLATE

Food waste has a big impact on climate change. If it ends up in a landfill site, it will rot and release methane (a damaging greenhouse gas) into the environment. So, only take what you need, enjoy your food and clean your plate.

3

TURN DOWN THE HEAT

If you're cold, think about wrapping up and putting on a jumper, rather than turning the thermostat up. This saves energy and carbon.

4

GROW YOUR OWN

Growing your own fruits and vegetables will help prevent CO_2 emissions from trucks, planes and ships that your bring your food from far away.

5

PLANT A TREE

Planting a tree can help remove CO_2 from the atmosphere and help tackle climate change.

6

REDUCE

Reduce the waste you produce in your daily life. For example, by using a refillable water bottle or cup rather than buying a new plastic bottle each time.

7 RECYCLE AND REUSE

Recycle your waste and think about using second-hand items or swapping things you no longer want rather than buy new.

8 WALK, RIDE OR TAKE THE BUS

If it's safe, then consider walking, cycling and taking the bus for short trips rather than going by car.

9 SAVE WATER

Consider how much water you need when washing and brushing your teeth. Try not to waste water by leaving the tap running too long.

10 SPREAD THE WORD

Encourage your friends, family, neighbours and teachers to do their bit and become earth warriors too!

ACKNOWLEDGEMENTS

In 2012, I naively set off on a journey to write a children's book.

What you hold in your hands is the product of a six-year adventure with highs and lows, twists and turns and tortuous times. But I've finally arrived at the end of my journey, and I'm pleased to be able to share this story with the world.

Writing this book would not have been possible without the support, advice and encouragement of lots of different people. I am indebted to all of them.

In particular, I would like to thank Shelley Instone, Bella Pearson, Rachel Faulkner, Jenny Jacoby, Leonora Bulbeck, Jennie Roman and Jane Burnard for their editorial advice and helping me to become a better writer.

Thank you to my beta readers for reviewing early versions of the manuscript, namely: Heidi Folland, Charlotte Hall, Cieran Gunn, Eleanor Cookdale and Harrison Berrill.

I bored lots of people talking about this project and I am grateful to the following individuals for their patience and tolerance! Thank you to Elena Paffumi, Michele De Gennaro, Michelle Kendall, Monique Bense, Adrian O'Connell, Monica Padella, Andrew Cottam and Wouter Heynderickx.

I would have given up a long time ago if it were not for my writing buddy Sam Haward. Thank you, Sam, for being so positive and annoyingly always right. Also, a big thank you to my poor sister, Michelene Pardington, who read the manuscript so many times she could recite it in her sleep!

I feel honoured to have had the opportunity to collaborate with the marvellous Mandy Norman and Mark Beech on the cover and text design. They have done a splendid job! Thank you also to Hannah Cooper for helping me let the world know about this story.

I never set out to write a book with an environmental theme. But I am glad I did as it was the most natural thing to do after working with a tribe of earth warriors for the last twenty years. Thank you to all my earth warrior colleagues at the Stockholm Environment Institute for their inspiration, dedication and efforts to achieve a better planet for all of us. Special thanks to Steve Cinderby, Dieter Schwela, Howard Cambridge and his flip-flops!

Enormous hugs and kisses to my dear wife, Heidi, and my daughter, Arabella, for their love, support and allowing me to be distracted by this story. I'm grateful for Heidi's continuous advice and suggestions – I couldn't have done it without her!

Finally, thank you to you the reader of this book. I hope you enjoyed it. If you did, then please tell others about it!

Gary Haq is an earth warrior whose day job is saving the planet. He is an associate researcher at a prestigious global environmental think tank and a research scientist at a European research centre. He tries his best to be the change he wants to see in the world and hopes to inspire others with his stories. When he's not involved in his own eco-adventures, he likes to write, read, learn languages and explore new cultures. Gary lives with his wife and young daughter, and spends his time between York, England and Laveno, Italy.

www.garyhaqwrites.com

@drgaryhaq